MY GIRL

JACK JORDAN

First published in paperback and eBook in 2016

First edition.

Typeset by Hope Services (Abingdon) Ltd.

Printed in Britain, fulfilled by Amazon.

ISBN: 978-1532815386

Also by Jack Jordan:

Anything for Her

Nanny Pam, thank you for all of the bedtime stories that you told me as a child, and for making them so funny that our faces hurt from smiling and our bellies ached from laughing. I cherish all of our memories, and I love you with all my heart.

I

1

For the first few seconds after she woke, Paige Dawson lived in a world where her husband Ryan was snoring lightly beside her, and her daughter Chloe was sleeping peacefully in the next room. When reality slowly trickled in, she instantly wanted to return to sleep – to forget they were dead – to stop the tears from rolling down her cheeks.

As her eyes adjusted to the room, she coughed violently. Stale smoke sat in the air. Worn clothes lay crumpled on the living room floor, smelling of damp and old sweat. Cigarette ash had been trodden into the carpet. A photo frame faced the ceiling. Ryan smiled from behind the cracked glass; a time when he was happy – before he slashed his wrists.

Get up. You need to get up.

She reached down to the carpet and patted around the mess in the dark until she found the tray of tablets. It shook in her hands as she popped each pill through the foil: *one, two, three.* She placed them on her dry tongue, picked up the half-empty wine bottle from the floor and took a swig. The wine was warm, but it did the job. The diazepam would kick in soon.

As she sat up, pain exploded in her temples. She lit a cigarette, cringed with the first toke, and stared at the daylight creeping from behind the closed curtains. The real world was taunting her: *you can't hide away from me forever.*

The smell of sick filled the house. How long it had been in the house with her: a night? A week? She wondered if there would be blood in it again.

What would Chloe think if she saw me like this?

Chloe would have been twenty-four years old by now. Her severed arm had been found in the river, her fourteen-year-old fingertips breaking through the surface. They never found the rest of her body, nor did they find the person who killed her. The forensics team had tested her blood: she had been alive when her murderer began chopping her up.

The diazepam wasn't working fast enough. She could still feel the painful void in her chest; she could still see her husband's blood swirling around in the bathwater. If she closed her eyes, Ryan's lifeless eyes flashed in front of hers.

She snatched the packet of codeine from the side table and swallowed two tablets with more wine.

When she lifted the cigarette to her lips, she found it wasn't there. She peered over the edge of the sofa and saw the cigarette burning a black hole into the carpet.

Maybe the diazepam is working.

She picked up the cigarette, spat on the blackened carpet, and gave it a rub with her finger, as though she had kissed a child's plastered graze. *There. All better.*

She spotted Ryan watching her from the mess on the ground, his lips frozen in an eternal smile.

However hard she tried, she couldn't remember the last time she kissed those lips. She couldn't remember when the kisses stopped, or when the distance started.

She shook the thought from her head and stumbled into the kitchen.

The bin was bulging with weeks of waste. Empty wine bottles lined the wall by the back door. Loud, languid flies buzzed around in hopeless circles. An uneaten meal sat in a pan on the stove, discoloured and congealed. She couldn't even remember cooking it, let alone forgetting to eat it.

The last time she had looked into Ryan's eyes while he was alive, he had been pinning her to the floor with his body as he forced a slice of bread into her mouth. His frustrated tears fell onto her face as he begged her to eat. He only stopped when the bread lodged in her throat. He had freed the blockage with fingers bent like a fishhook and then, as she gasped for air, he had sobbed from where he lay on the carpet, with bits of bread and saliva coating his fingers.

She wasn't starving herself – she just forgot to eat.

The sound of the key turning in the lock made her jolt. Her mother-in-law gasped. Shame turned in Paige's gut.

Greta stood in the doorway with her eyes on the mess. 'Paige, this is…'

'I was about to clean up,' she replied as she returned to the living room.

Greta placed her bags by the door. She looked reluctant to close it, to say goodbye to the fresh air, but when she did, it slammed.

'How could you let it get this bad?'

Greta threw open the curtains. Paige squinted as daylight burst into the room.

'Are those *burns* on the carpet?'

As Greta rifled through the mess, Paige wondered how the woman before her held herself together. Her hair had been set at the salon, her make-up was perfect, her clothes were ironed and fresh. No one would have known that her only son had committed suicide just two months before.

'I expected better from you, Paige.'

Paige glanced at herself in the mirror above the fireplace and saw greasy auburn hair, streaks of mascara hardened on her cheeks, the stained nightgown stuck to her body with sweat. She looked older than her forty-two years.

'I don't know why, but I had a feeling you might have changed the locks.'

'I wouldn't do that.'

Greta spotted the photo of Ryan, hidden beneath the cracks in the glass. She sighed and took it in her hands. For a moment her frown disappeared, and she looked almost beautiful. She stood the photo frame on the coffee table and looked back to Paige. The frown immediately returned.

'Not up to cleaning yet?' Greta asked, as she picked up her bags and carried them into the kitchen.

'I've got other things on my mind,' Paige replied, following her into the kitchen.

'Shall I? I've done your food shopping, so I might as well do your cleaning.'

Paige held her resentment back. 'I was just heading out.'

'Presumably after you've showered.'

She looked Paige up and down again.

'Obviously.'

'I will clean while you're out, then.'

'If that would please you, Greta.'

'It would. Ryan would want me to look out for you.'

'Thanks.'

Greta looked around the mess for other aspects to criticise. Paige waited patiently, longing to be alone.

'Are you sleeping on the sofa?'

'For now.'

'Imagine if one of your neighbours should walk past and see you.'

Greta went into the living room to stare at the mess again, lost at where to start. Paige followed behind her.

'I don't care what people think of me.'

'Clearly. I can't remember the last time I saw you clean and dressed.'

'That's the thing with being a widow, you focus on the death of your partner, rather than what people think of you.'

'Well, if I were you—'

'But you aren't, Greta.'

They stared at each other, like two cats about to fight. They stood in silence for a while, their eyes locked.

'You said you were off out?'

'Doctor's appointment.'

'Who is it you see?'

'Dr Abdullah.'

'Ah yes, the Muslim fellow. I prefer Dr Phillips. She's Christian.'

'Dr Abdullah is a Christian, too, I believe.'

'Really? Still, I prefer Sally. She has a kind air about her, and presents herself well.' Greta looked her up and down as she spoke.

'Well, I'll leave you to it.'

'Yes. I'd better start cleaning, before this place becomes infested with rats.' Greta picked up an ashtray from the coffee table. 'Must you really smoke in the house? Ryan would have never allowed it.'

'Well Ryan's dead now, isn't he? So I'll smoke in my house if I want to.'

Greta flinched, but held her tongue.

'Thanks for the food,' Paige said, and made for the stairs.

The moment she got upstairs, she turned on the shower and retrieved the bottle of wine she had hidden under her bed. She certainly wasn't going to step out into the real world without help.

Paige returned to the bathroom and locked the door behind her. She peeled off the nightgown that stuck to her like a second skin, sat on the toilet and drank wine straight from the bottle as steam filled the room. She stared at the bath and saw Ryan's lifeless body lying in the red water, his vacant eyes locked on hers. Paige clenched her eyes shut and shook her head.

He's not real. He's gone.

When she opened her eyes again, the bath was empty. Ryan was gone.

She checked her urine: blood again. She flushed the blood from the toilet, and the thought from her mind. She couldn't think about that right now.

As she breathed in the thick, hot mist, and drank warm wine from the bottle, she began to cry silent tears: she could never escape the fact that she was the mother of a murdered child and wife to a dead man.

2

Paige wondered if the other people in the waiting room knew that she had been drinking. The receptionist had looked her up and down as she walked in, a little unsteady on her feet.

The man sitting next to her broke into a coughing fit until he was red in the face. She leaned away from him and looked up at the noticeboard, hoping to see her name.

A toddler was playing with some toys in the corner. Paige watched her intently, seeking out similarities between her and Chloe when she was that age.

The child's mother stroked her daughter's hair, picked her up and held her close. Paige blushed. She had been staring again.

The man next to her coughed again, almost retching, with raised veins protruding from his neck. The electronic noticeboard beeped and her name appeared.

Paige grabbed her bag and hurried towards the doctor's office, with the heat of the mother's glare on her back.

She knocked on the door, and heard him call for her to enter.

Dr Abdullah had been treating Paige and her family for over fifteen years. He had watched the family dwindle down to one.

Sitting with his back to a small window overlooking the car park, Dr Abdullah peered over his glasses and smiled. His bronze, aged skin contrasted with his white beard and hair. His gut protruded over his belt, straining the buttons on his white shirt.

She decided not to tell him about the blood in her urine. Not him. Anyone but him.

'Paige, how are you?'

'Fine,' she replied as she sat down.

'I'm sorry for what you're going through, without Ryan.'

'It's fine.'

Why do I say that? Of course it's not fine.

'How are you coping? Do you think you need your dosage upped again?'

'Not yet.'

'Are you here for a refill?'

'Yes.'

'That's sooner than usual.'

'I'm in more pain than usual.'

'I see.'

He pulled up her record on the computer screen.

Anxiety sat in her stomach. She hated this bit. She couldn't wait to be back home on the sofa where she felt safe. Where the wine was.

The diazepam was prescribed for anxiety, while the codeine was for a back injury that she'd made up for the drugs. Both of them kept up the lie – it was in both of their best interests.

'I can only prescribe you sixty of each, and that's pushing it.'

'Sure. Whatever.'

A machine whirled as the prescription began to print. Dr Abdullah took out six extra packets of pills from his drawer, placed them on the desk, and began to untie his belt.

'The blinds,' she said.

'Oh yes,' he laughed. 'That wouldn't do, would it?'

He spun around in his chair and closed the blinds as Paige snatched the pills from the desk and pushed them deep into her bag. He put her prescription on the desk with one hand, and unzipped his flies with the other.

Paige got on her knees, tasted him in her mouth, and shuddered with shame.

3

Paige walked from the GP surgery to the therapist's office in Maidstone town centre. She felt sick from the taste of him, and wondered if people could tell that she'd just given her doctor a blow job for extra drugs. Could they see the shame in her eyes? Could they smell him on her breath?

She needed a drink. She made a beeline for the pub opposite the therapist's office. It was dark and depressing inside. Old men sat in booths with pints of local ale. The carpet belonged to the 1970s and the windows were dirty and smeared.

'Large Pinot Grigio,' she said to the barman, without meeting his eye.

She needed to rid the taste of the doctor from her mouth. He had lasted longer this time. Usually it was over in five minutes or so. Today, she had worked on him until her jaw ached. She thought of Dr Abdullah's climax hitting the roof of her mouth, the sour taste, the warmth, the shame.

She took the glass of wine from the barman's hand before the glass could even touch the bar.

Imagine what Chloe would think.

She shook the thought from her head.

I wouldn't need the pills so badly if she hadn't been killed, would I?

She sat at the bar in silence, sipping the wine quickly as though someone was about to take it from her.

To her left, a man sat hunched over his pint. The whites of his eyes were a rotten yellow, and the wrinkles on his face were so deep that they looked as though they had been cut with a razor. He didn't look up when the door opened – he wasn't expecting company. He was there for the alcohol and nothing more. They were the same.

The man looked up and caught her staring. A smirk turned the corners of his mouth. A tooth was missing from his grin.

Paige looked down at her glass, which trembled in her hand. Embarrassment flared through her and her cheeks felt hot. She longed for him to look away, to forget her. She sensed him coming towards her and willed herself to stop shaking.

'Paige.'

She snapped around to the sound of her name. Her father was standing in the doorway of the pub.

'How'd I know to find you in here? I've been waiting outside for ten minutes. Come on.'

She had never been so happy to see her father. The man backed away as she downed her drink and headed for the door.

'You didn't have to come,' she said as she left the pub and walked to the opposite side of the road with him.

'I did. I need to know you're serious, Paige. That you're going to go to get the help you need.'

Her father was short, overweight, and walked with a limp, putting all of the weight on his better hip. He smelt of cigars and port.

'I feel like a child,' she said, as they entered the building and stood before the lift.

'You're *my* child. Always will be.'

They waited for the lift to travel to the ground floor.

Both of them had been widowed, but Paige's mother hadn't died by her own hand – cancer had eaten away at her from the inside a long time ago.

'Who was that man?' he asked.

'Doesn't matter.'

The doors opened and they entered the lift. Her father pressed the button for the third floor. Paige's chest tightened as the doors closed and she watched her last chance of escape vanish.

'So Robin Higgins is the therapist,' he said. 'Came highly recommended by a friend.'

The smell of port stalked his breath.

'You ever thought of therapy, Dad?'

'No one's perfect. I'm beyond help. You still have time to turn your life around.'

'Don't see the point.'

'Just try for me, all right?'

She nodded. The doors opened on the third floor.

The reception desk was on the right, the waiting room in front, and a long corridor trailed off from the left.

As her dad went to the reception desk, Paige sat down in the waiting area. There were two other people waiting to be seen. She couldn't help but wonder what their problems were.

I bet they aren't as screwed up as I am.

Her father sat down next to her, took the folded newspaper from under his arm and began to read.

Despite the wine, she could still taste the doctor. She couldn't help but wonder what her father would think of her if he knew what she had been doing before she met him. He would never be able to look her in the eye again.

'Is this expensive? I don't want you spending loads of money on me.'

'Nothing I can't handle. I want to do this for you.'

They waited in silence. Paige wondered if she could get away with popping a pill in her mouth without her father noticing.

One of the men in the waiting area was dressed in

an expensive-looking suit. Paige wondered how it felt to have a job like his. Did he feel pride? Did his life have more value because of it? Her unemployment always filled her with shame. It wasn't that she couldn't get a job – she just never managed to keep one for very long.

An attractive man emerged from the hallway and whispered something to the receptionist over the desk, before walking towards the waiting area.

'Paige Dawson?'

She snapped her head towards her father. *A man?*

'She's here,' her dad said. He turned to look at her. 'Be good. I'll be right here.'

Instantly shaking, she stood and walked off with the man.

Robin. I thought it was a woman. I don't want a man. I don't want this.

'Great to meet you,' he said through a smile as they walked down the hall. 'My office is just down here.'

He opened a door with his name on it, that unisex name that she already hated for tricking her, and held the door open for her to enter.

The room was spacious and light, yet comforting from the warm coloured fabrics on the chairs and the cushions. Paige didn't like the comforting colours; it felt like a trap: *you're safe in here. Now tell me all of your dirty secrets.*

'I need to use the bathroom,' she said.

'No problem. The toilets are at the end of the hall. I'll put the kettle on. Tea or coffee?'

'Coffee. Black, no sugar.'

Robin nodded and headed down the hallway. Paige went in the opposite direction for the bathroom. Beside the toilet door was a fire exit. She looked down the hall and watched Robin as he walked in the opposite direction and out of sight. The door to the fire exit slammed against the wall as she ran down the stairs.

4

Paige woke up in the police cell with a pounding headache.

It was a small cell, with a bed built into the wall and a blue plastic mattress. The laces had been removed from her shoes, along with her belt and her wedding ring. She got up, aching all over, and walked barefoot on the cold floor to the silver toilet in the corner of the cell. A security camera moved when she moved.

What the hell did I do?

When she drank, she often suffered from blackouts – dark, taunting gaps in her memory – but this was the first time she had woken up in a police cell.

You went back to the pub. You walked home. You drank some more.

Slowly, she began to remember.

She looked down at herself and saw that she was covered in dry mud, which came off in thick flakes. She remembered hearing the gravel hitting the bottom of the car as she raced towards Ryan's gravestone. She had barely been able to see where she was going through the tears in her eyes. She remembered lurching forward with the impact of the crash and seeing the world outside the windscreen jolt upwards, before being thrown back into her seat as the car mounted the headstone. The next thing she remembered was lying on Chloe's grave next to Ryan's – with the car engine still running, lights still on, wheels still spinning – sobbing into the grass and mud. She had woken again to see a police officer checking her pulse. He had been out of breath, talking on his radio, checking Paige over for injuries. She couldn't remember anymore.

Paige promised herself never to drink again, but in the same moment she wondered how long it would be until she was at home, pouring herself another glass.

A polystyrene plate sat on the floor in front of the door offering a cold, stale sandwich that she had refused to eat the night before. She had drunk the tea they offered: it had burned her tongue. Just as she was considering eating the sandwich, the hatch on the door opened.

A police officer peered inside the cell, stared at her, and then closed the hatch again before opening the door.

'You've been granted bail. Your lift is here, too.'

When asked for a next of kin the night before, she had given them Ryan's details, until she remembered he was dead. She gave them Maxim's name and phone number instead. Now that she remembered, she considered asking to stay in the cell so she didn't have to face Maxim. But the promise of a drink was greater than her dread of her brother, so she slipped her feet into her shoes and followed the officer.

The walk to the reception desk was humiliating. Her shoes were loose without laces, so she had to drag her feet along the floor like a child waiting to grow into her new shoes. She almost tripped and had to grab the arm of the officer, who flinched at her touch.

The police officer led her to the reception desk and stood at her side. The custody officer behind the desk didn't smile back at her.

'Do you remember much of last night?' she asked.

Paige shook her head. The custody officer looked familiar. Then she remembered: they had gone to school together. Samantha – that was her name. Samantha had a career, a ring on her finger, probably a few kids. They couldn't have turned out more different. Paige couldn't look Samantha in the eye. The embarrassment was just too great.

'You've been charged with reckless driving under section 2 of the Road Traffic Act 1988, driving under the influence of alcohol under section 4 of Road Traffic Act 1988, criminal damage and vandalism of private property under section 1 of the Criminal Damage Act

1971, and drunk and disorderly behaviour under the Criminal Justice Act 1967.'

Paige had to remind herself to breathe. She must have looked clueless, because Samantha sighed.

'You drove through the gates of the cemetery, knocked down a wall, and destroyed a gravestone.'

Not just any gravestone, Paige thought. *Ryan's.*

'You've been granted bail. You will need to attend the court hearing on the twenty-third of November. Failure to attend may see a warrant being issued for your arrest and further charges being brought against you. Do you understand?'

Paige nodded furiously.

'I recommend you consult with a solicitor soon. Everything you need to know about financial aid and finding a solicitor is in this pack.'

Samantha pushed a pile of papers towards her. Paige stared at it for a few seconds, overwhelmed. She signed loads of forms without reading them. Her hands were shaking so badly that her signature was nothing but a scribble. The whole time, she could feel her brother's stare burning into her back. Samantha kept talking. Paige nodded along as she put the laces back into her shoes. She took her belongings out of the plastic bags they had been stored in overnight and pulled the pile of papers close to her chest.

'Who else were you with?' Samantha asked.

'Pardon?'

'The other car. Were you being chased?'

'What other car?'

Paige looked at the officer, bewildered. The officer stared back at her.

'There was another car in the graveyard.'

'Who was driving it?'

'We don't know.'

'Well I don't, either.'

Paige heard her brother sigh behind her and the sound of his foot tapping impatiently on the hard floor. Samantha noticed it too.

'Call us if you remember anything.'

Paige nodded.

Keeping her head down, she walked over to Maxim. Her cheeks felt hot.

Maxim's black hair was turning grey, and his skin looked loose and tired. The clerical collar made him look even older.

'I'll pay you back for the bail money.'

'You think I'm angry about that?'

'I've learnt my lesson.'

'You've said that so many times before.'

'Well, I mean it this time.'

'Come on.'

They left the station, and Paige immediately lit a cigarette and took a deep drag.

Maxim looked tired. She wondered what time they had called him. His eyelids were puffy.

'You need to get it together, Paige.'

She was too ashamed to speak.

'Your husband died. So did your daughter. It's awful. But that doesn't mean you can drive around drunk and cause havoc.'

'I know. I'm sorry.'

'*Do* you know? You've been pulling stunts like this for ten years. It's time to snap out of it. You're going to end up killing yourself.'

A flash of her husband dead in the bath invaded her mind. Blood. So much blood.

'Can you just take me home?'

'Why did you do that? Destroy Ryan's grave?'

She smoked her cigarette, revealing nothing.

He left me on my own. He didn't even say goodbye.

'I've been so patient with you, Paige, but now I think you need some tough love. *Let. It. Go.* You can't change the past. You can't bring them back. But you can make a life for yourself: get a job, make friends, be happy. Chloe wouldn't want you to live like this.'

She took one last drag on her cigarette before dropping it to the ground and killing it with the stamp of her foot.

'You can tell me what to do with my life when you find your only child's body parts in a river. You get to judge me when *your* partner kills himself where only you will find him. You can give me tough love when you have even the *slightest* idea of what I'm going through.'

'I can't sleep at night because I'm so worried about you. I wake up in the middle of the night wondering if you're safe or dead somewhere. I have my own problems, thanks to you. Maybe you should have some more consideration for the people that are still here, who love you and need you to be safe.'

'I never asked you to worry about me. I don't want your pity or your criticism. I want to be left alone.'

'So you can eventually kill yourself?'

'Of course not.'

'Well that's what you're going to end up doing, whether you mean to or not. Or you'll end up in prison. Wake up, Paige. You're a mess.'

'Your life isn't so damn perfect. At least I know who I am.'

'What is that supposed to mean?'

'You haven't had a girlfriend in your entire life. Just come out, Maxim. Stop hiding behind that dog collar.'

'I'm not gay.'

'Well pull your finger out and get a girlfriend. All you do is read the damn Bible and piss me off.'

'Maybe I could settle down and be happy if I wasn't so worried about you all the time. Maybe you can do us both a favour by sorting your life out.'

'Don't blame your sorry life on me.'

'And what about Dad? If you carry on the way you are, he'll have another heart attack.'

That hit her hard, like a blow to the chest. She didn't speak for a moment.

'Paige, I'm sorry…'

'I just want to go home. Please, just take me home.'

*　　*　　*

Maxim took the long route home, down the country lanes, which gave both of them time to calm down. As the car pulled up outside the house, the two of them were silent.

Paige looked at the house, wedged between the neighbouring houses along the terraced street, and reminded herself that it was just *her* home now, not *theirs*. She wouldn't hear Chloe's music drifting down the stairs, or walk in to the smell of Ryan's cooking. Nothing awaited her but silence and memories of the dead.

'I'll pay you back,' she said, opening the passenger door. 'Thanks for coming to get me.'

Before Maxim could reply, she shut the car door and searched for her keys in her bag.

'I made you some dinners,' he called out.

She turned around to see her brother shutting the car door and clutching numerous plastic containers.

'I made them yesterday. Just throw them in the freezer and heat them up when you're hungry.'

A grateful smile crept onto her face.

'Thank you,' she said as she took them from him.

'You're looking thin in the face, so heat one up the second you get in.'

'I will.'

'You can always stay with me,' he said.

'I need to do this on my own. I can't have people looking after me forever.'

He nodded and headed back to the car.

'You'll make someone very happy one day, Maxim. Don't leave it until it's too late.'

He smiled and sat behind the steering wheel.

She put the key into the lock and went inside.

The house reeked of stale smoke and misery, but the living room was spotless. The kitchen was gleaming, and fresh laundry was ironed and folded neatly in the washing basket. There was a sticky note from Greta on the fridge.

Try not to let it get so bad again, Paige.

Paige screwed up the note and threw it in the bin.

She sat down at the breakfast table with a fork and ate one of Maxim's meals, cold. After half a portion, she put the dish in the fridge and poured herself a large wine. It looked as though she had stocked up on Pinot before she went driving around town and crashing into headstones. She popped six pills into her palm and swallowed them down in one go.

Paige went back into the living room with her glass and considered sleeping on the sofa again. Ryan's scent still lingered on the bed sheets. His unfinished book was still on the bedside table, his reading glasses resting on top. His clothes still hung on his side of the wardrobe.

She headed upstairs and caught a glimpse of the bath she had found him in. Blood was running down the bath panel and creeping between the tiles on the floor.

It's not real. It's all in your mind.

She snatched her eyes away and stopped outside Chloe's door. She found herself turning the handle and stepped inside.

The smell of her filled Paige's nostrils and warmed her heart. She quickly closed the door behind her, to stop the scent from escaping. The bed was still made. The curtains were open. Photos were stuck all over the walls like a collage: friends, family, a poster of some hunky actor that Paige could never name. Paige sat on the bed and drained her glass. It hurt remembering Chloe, being surrounded by her. Ten years had passed since Chloe had been taken from her – snatched from the roadside as she walked home from school – but to Paige, it felt like yesterday.

'Who killed you, Chloe?' she said into the room. 'What happened to you?'

Tears stung at her eyes. She inhaled her daughter's sweet scent until she sobbed.

'I miss you every minute of every day. I feel like a part of me died with you. I want to move on, to try and be happy, but I can't. I can't be happy without you.'

She lay down on the bed, clutched her daughter's pillow to her chest, and cried herself to sleep.

5

Paige was beckoned from her slumber by the sound of Chloe's voice.

It can't be her. I must still be dreaming.

Chloe was laughing, a young child's laugh. She was calling for her father.

They're dead. This is a dream. I'll wake up soon.

And then she heard her own voice. She almost didn't recognise it – it sounded so happy, so free.

Paige sat up and looked around Chloe's bedroom in search of her, in search of Ryan. The small television was on, with a young Chloe on the screen, ghostly behind the dust. Paige hadn't watched their home videos in a long time. Seeing her daughter's beaming smile and shimmering red hair, and hearing her voice and her laugh, it was all too much, like a knife to her heart.

The video footage was from their trip to Majorca in the summer of 1997. Paige had been holding the camera, and her younger, happier voice could be heard commentating on the scene. Chloe wore a pink one-piece, and her red hair was soaked and plastered to her head and neck; she would have been about eight years old then. Ryan was noticeably younger, slimmer, happier. His nose was burnt and red, and his shoulders were peeling. They were taking it in turns to dive into the pool under the blazing hot sun while Paige scored the dives out of ten. She let Chloe win most times.

Tears ran down Paige's cheeks as she watched the footage, but she couldn't seem to draw her eyes away.

Stop watching it. You're only hurting yourself.

She hugged Chloe's pillow to her chest as though it were Chloe in her arms.

Paige watched the footage right to the end. Only when the tape turned itself off, bringing her back to the present, did she wonder how it had come to play in the first place.

I didn't put the tape on. I came up here and fell asleep on the bed. I didn't hunt for the tape and play it... did I?

Her memory was awful after she'd been drinking, like a broken film reel. Whole segments of time were missing, fuzzy, unsalvageable. In fact, her recollection of most her life seemed to be full of taunting gaps, so that she only had a handful of memories to look back on. She barely remembered her childhood, although she was glad she wouldn't have to live it again. Maybe it was a good thing she couldn't remember.

But she had no recollection of putting the tape on to play.

You live in this house on your own now. Who else could have done it?

She smelt the pillow, hoping to find Chloe's scent still there, and not replaced with the stench of stale cigarettes and wine. It was there, but it was faint. She got up before she did more damage and headed downstairs.

She popped two pills for the wine-induced headache, made herself coffee and sat down on the sofa. It was half seven in the morning and still dark outside.

'OPEN THIS DOOR, NOW!' her father bellowed, as he banged on the front door with his fist.

She jolted and spilled the coffee down her front. She rushed to the door and let him in. Anger seemed to radiate from him. She shut the door behind him.

'What the *hell* were you thinking?'

'I'm sorry I left the therapy session, I couldn't…'

'It's not about that. That's the last thing on my mind.'

It took her a moment to remember: the graveyard, the police station.

'I'm sorry, I was—'

'Drunk. Of course you were. You always are.' He paced the room, shaking, breathing hard. 'This has got to stop, Paige. You can't keep going on like this. Do you want me to have another heart attack?'

'Of course not.'

'Then stop stressing me out!'

'I don't know what I was thinking. I *wasn't* thinking.'

'Just because Ryan's dead, it doesn't mean that you get to put yourself at risk now. People still care about you. *I* still care about you.' His whole frame was shaking. 'I wake up some nights, wondering if you're asleep in your bed or dead in a ditch somewhere. How would I know? How would anybody know?'

Paige hadn't seen her father so angry. Breathless, he rummaged around in his pocket and pulled out an inhaler. He pumped it twice into his mouth.

'Dad, sit down.'

'I don't want to sit down.'

'*Sit down.*'

They sat on the sofa and she took her father's hand in hers. Both of them were shaking.

'What am I going to do with you?'

He looked her at with such desperation in his eyes.

'Dad, I'm sorry. I didn't know you got like this.'

'Of course I do: you're my daughter. I love you. I worry about you all the time.'

'I'm sorry.'

Paige rested her head on his shoulder.

'How do you do that?'

'Do what?'

'Calm me down when I'm so angry with you?'

She couldn't help but smile; she rubbed the back of his hand with her thumb.

The phone in Ryan's office began to ring upstairs. Paige had disconnected it, meaning Greta must have meddled with it. Paige sat still, waiting for the call to end.

'Aren't you going to answer it?'

'And tell every caller that my husband is dead?'

'They need to know.'

'And I need peace.'

They sat listening to the phone ring until it stopped, and the house fell silent again.

'You're right. You do deserve peace. Let's sort out his office – get rid of it all.'

But he might need it, Paige thought, before she remembered that Ryan wouldn't be coming back.

'I've got a good shredder at home. I could spend my evenings shredding all of the documents in those cabinets. It would give me something to do.'

She didn't feel up to it, but as she looked into her father's patient eyes, she nodded.

'Great. I'll go for a slash and then we'll get started.'

Paige watched as her father climbed the stairs. The moment he was out of sight, she rushed into the kitchen, poured a glass of wine, and took two diazepam tablets. She listened to her father drumming into the toilet bowl above her, and gulped down the last of the wine as he flushed the toilet.

*   *   *

Ryan's office was set up in the smallest bedroom in the house. His desk faced the window, which looked out over the long, overgrown garden. His closed laptop was layered with dust, and an old coffee cup had mould growing inside it. Along the wall was row of filing cabinets, far too big for the room.

Paige hadn't let his clients know that their accountant was dead. His inbox was probably filled with frustrated enquiries. She couldn't face them – not yet.

Her dad carried stacks of documents down the stairs and out to his car after Paige had had a quick look at them in case they ought to be kept. By dinnertime they had got through all four cabinets.

Paige began to look through the drawers in Ryan's desk. Each drawer she opened was freakishly neat, the contents arranged according to size. She began throwing the notepads, the pens, the packs of sticky notes, and the business cards into a black bin bag. She just wanted to get rid of everything. She had no idea how she was going to use the room once everything was gone.

Her father appeared behind her, out of breath, picked up the last stack of papers, and took them down to the car.

She was about to close the last drawer when she spotted a loose panel at the bottom. A shadow in the corner of the drawer suggested there was something underneath. She used her nails to prise up the corner of the panel. Lying underneath was a black handgun and an old, brick-like phone.

'Is that everything?'

She slammed the drawer shut.

'Yeah.'

'I'll call my friend and sort out a date and time to get these cabinets out of here. He'll get you a good price. Do you want him to take the desk, too?'

'No!' she replied, too quickly. Her father frowned. 'I'll keep it. The room would look odd without it.'

'All right then. So, are you going to make your dad a cup of tea for all of his hard work?'

She nodded and forced a smile.

Her father grinned and went down the stairs, talking away to her. Paige got up from the desk chair to follow him, but stopped at the doorway. She turned and looked back at the desk.

Why had Ryan needed a gun?

6

Paige looked down at the river with tears in her eyes. The water was murky and dark at dusk. Chloe had always been afraid of the dark.

Sitting on the path by the riverbank, she brought the wine bottle to her lips and took a swig.

The thought of someone cutting up her daughter's body and scattering her in the river never failed to bring tears to Paige's eyes. She wondered how much of her was still down there, hidden beneath reeds and scum, missed by the police divers all those years ago. She told herself to stop going there, to refrain from looking down at the water and imagining what had happened; but still, she found herself there a lot. Tonight though, she had other thoughts plaguing her mind.

Ryan had owned a gun.

She couldn't understand how he would have got hold of a gun, or why he would need one at all. Having a gun of his own went against everything he believed in. Whenever shootings in America were on the news, his nostrils would flare and his jaw would clench. *Take the damn guns away and you won't have cops gunning down kids or teens going on killing sprees! First amendment my arse. They're deadly weapons, not damn toys. Grow up and protect your own people!*

And then he had acquired a gun of his own.

He hadn't used the gun to end his life; he'd used a razor for that. So why else would he need a gun? Did he want to shoot Chloe's murderer? If the police couldn't pin down her killer, how could he?

She took another swig of wine.

None of it would matter if she went to prison. The thought of appearing in court made bile climb her throat. She had gone too far this time.

The thought of prison and the gun hidden in her house compelled her to drain the rest of the wine. She threw the empty bottle in the river, and watched it follow the current for a moment before it sank into the darkness.

The sun had set and night filled the sky. She couldn't bear to leave Chloe down there in the dark.

'Goodnight, my darling,' she whispered, and struggled to her feet.

As she stood and turned to leave, she lost her balance, fell backwards, and plunged into the darkness. Water poured into her mouth and up her nose just as she began to scream. She thrashed beneath the surface, choking on the dark water and pulling at the reeds that tangled around her legs. Chloe's body flashed before her eyes: a bloody arm, her severed head with her mouth frozen mid-scream. River water filled her lungs as she sobbed. She clawed at the water and forced herself upwards until she broke the surface, coughing up the dirty water. She snatched the edge of the path by the river and dragged herself up, her clothes drenched and pulling her down with the weight. She lay on the path and coughed up the black water as tears streamed from her eyes.

*　　*　　*

Blind drunk and soaking wet, Paige stumbled into the house. As she tried to strip off the clothes that clung to her body, she tripped on her jeans and slammed face-first onto the floor.

The room was dark with the night. She lay there for a moment with her face to the side, utterly defeated. From the floor, she noticed a change in the room. She struggled to pinpoint it at first.

Where are Ryan's books?

She hadn't got rid of them – she wouldn't have. Couldn't have.

She looked up at the bookcase, bare of belongings. His CDs weren't there either.

Who would do this?

Her stomach clenched like a fist and sent bile hissing up her throat. Greta.

How dare she!

She struggled to her feet, buttoned up her jeans and staggered upstairs. Immediately she noticed that Ryan's book and reading glasses were no longer on his bedside table. She opened his drawer. Empty.

'That bitch!'

She yanked open the wardrobe doors. Ryan's side only stored bare hangers, which rattled against each other as she slammed the doors shut. She covered her face with her hands and tried to digest her anger. Hot, furious tears stung her eyes. Dirty water dripped from her hair and clothes, and seeped into the carpet.

How dare she come into my home and take his stuff! How could she?

Paige paced the room, trying to think of a reason for Greta to do such a thing, to think she had the right to destroy Ryan's memory.

She wanted the belongings for herself. That's why. She couldn't stand not having anything to remember him by, so she took what was mine.

A new fear stopped her in her tracks.

Chloe's room.

Paige rushed out of her bedroom and barged into Chloe's. It hadn't been touched. She covered her face with quivering hands, too tense to sigh with relief.

I'll get his things back. She won't take them away from me.
She ran downstairs and stormed out of the house.

Marching through the village, anger swelled in her chest until she could hardly breathe. She shook all over as the cold night cooled the water on her skin and clothes.

The village of Loose was once a quaint community hidden in the beauty of Kent's hilly countryside, but the Dawsons had changed all that. Its reputation had been tarnished by Chloe's disappearance, stained with her blood. The murder had been featured in every national newspaper and on all of the television stations. The peaceful River Loose became the harbourer of body parts that belonged to an innocent fourteen-year-old girl. The friendly, close-knit community became hostile and suspicious. Everyone feared that the killer could still be among them. Seeing Paige about the village only reignited those fears: curtains were drawn, doors closed, dogs barked, whispers started. It was as though Paige were an angel of death.

When she reached her in-laws' house, she was ready to erupt. She banged on the door with her fist.

Ryan's father opened the door with a startled countenance.

'Paige… why are you all wet? What's wrong?'

'Your wife, that's what's wrong!'

Paige stormed past him and walked straight into the living room, treading dirty, wet footprints into the carpet.

'Where is she?'

'Greta, come in here!' he hollered down the hall, before following Paige into the living room. 'What's this about?'

Paige suddenly remembered the last time she saw Richard. It had been at Ryan's wake. She had got drunk and embarrassed herself. Richard drove her home. She did something unforgiveable.

'Greta took Ryan's stuff.'

'She *what?* When?'

'Today. I came home and saw his stuff was missing: clothes, books, cologne, everything.'

Greta walked in, drying her hands with a tea towel. She took in Paige's appearance. 'What on earth…'

'You!' Paige strode towards her, pointing a wet finger at her face. 'You took Ryan's things!'

'Why would I do that? Don't point, Paige. It's rude.'

'*I'm* rude? You come into my house like it's your own and take things that don't belong to you!'

'Is this true, Greta?' Richard asked.

'No! I didn't take anything!'

'Well who did, then?' Paige asked. 'Who else would come into my house and feel as though they have the right to do whatever they like?'

'Maybe your father did it,' Greta said.

'He doesn't have a key. You are the only person who has a key, which I would like back. Now.'

'This is ludicrous. Do you know that? All I've done is

try and support you, since the moment you and Ryan began your relationship. I don't deserve such rage!'

'You always stuck your nose into our business, judging every move we made. I couldn't feed my baby without you interfering, or do the washing without doing it wrong, or cook a meal without you turning your nose up at it. Ryan is dead – you don't have the right to bother me anymore!'

Greta had tears in her eyes and pursed lips. 'I tried to love you like a daughter.'

'Oh, please! You never thought I was good enough for Ryan.'

'Well, you weren't,' Richard said, silencing them both.

The three of them stood in silence. Greta wrung the tea towel in her hands.

'It's not as though you were faithful.'

'Stop it,' Paige said.

'What do you mean, Richard?'

'After the wake…'

'Richard, don't.'

'She tried to seduce me.'

'She *what*?'

'It's not how it sounds, Greta. I was emotional.'

'She touched me inappropriately.'

'I didn't want to be alone.'

'Where did she touch you? On the arm? The leg?'

'Richard, you don't need to…'

'Oh for God's sake, use your imagination, Greta.'

As the truth dawned on Greta, her jaw fell open. 'How could you? Why would you do that?'

Paige opened her mouth to apologise when Greta slapped her across the face.

'You get out of this house,' she said, as tears ran down her cheeks. 'You get out of this house and never come to us again!'

Greta walked out, sobbing, leaving Richard and Paige standing there staring silently at each other, Paige cupping her stinging cheek. A dark puddle surrounded her feet, seeping into the cream carpet. Greta came back into the room and threw the house key at Paige's feet. 'There's your key. Now leave.'

Feeling the heat of Greta's glare and Richard's disgust, Paige picked up the key and put it in her pocket.

'I'm… I'm sorry.'

Paige knew then that she had very few people left who loved her – that she had just destroyed a relationship that had spanned twenty years. Her last ties to Ryan had been cut.

She left without another word, her face hot with shame, and shut the front door behind her. It was only when she turned the key in her own front door that she wondered: *if Greta didn't take Ryan's things, then who did?*

7

Paige sat at a table by the window of the coffee shop. Raindrops raced down the glass and grey clouds smothered the sky. She was drenched from head to toe, with raindrops dripping from her hair. She shrugged out of her coat and placed her shaking hands around the warm coffee cup, wondering how long it would take for Detective Inspector Graham Balding to arrive.

Despite the dismal weather, sunglasses shielded her eyes. The day was too bright, and her headache was too great. She had drunk far too much last night, even for her. A drying pool of sick waited for her on the living room carpet – she couldn't face it yet, she would only vomit again at the stench. Spotting blood in it was normal for her now.

I'm not going mad. Someone is taunting me. I'm not doing this. I would remember. I'm not losing my mind.

Her hands trembled so badly that coffee spilled from

the cup as she lifted it to her lips. A young child watched her from another table. Embarrassed, she put the cup back on the saucer and hid her hands in her lap.

As DI Graham Balding entered the coffee shop, a damp gust of wind swept in with him. His dark brown face was moist with beads of rain. He lowered his hood, scanned the room for her, and nodded in greeting. While he paid for his coffee at the counter, Paige took in the changes to his appearance; the years hadn't been kind to him.

For every black hair on his head, there was a grey one; the skin on his face looked slack from age and sleepless nights. Paige wondered if he was dressed in the same suit she had last seen him wearing seven years ago.

The last time they met hadn't been a good experience for either of them. Paige had practically lunged across the desk at Balding when he told her and Ryan that Chloe's case was about to close unsolved. Ryan had simply stared ahead in shock, while Paige smacked the DI's chest and screamed belligerently.

'Do I need to get out my boxing gloves?' he said as he sat down opposite her.

'Not today.'

'Good. I'm surprised it's been so long.'

'I didn't think you would appreciate seeing my face again.'

'At least I know what to expect.' He took a sip of coffee. 'I'm sorry about Ryan.'

'It's fine.'

Why do I keep saying it's fine? Of course it's not bloody fine.

His lips turned into a closed smile, but his eyes were vacant. What horrors had he seen? What had drawn the life from his eyes?

'Strange things have been happening,' she said.

Balding watched her as he sipped his coffee.

'They are difficult to describe, because they make me sound crazy.'

'I'm not here to judge, I'm here to help.'

'Well, yesterday, Ryan's belongings went missing.'

'Missing?'

'Yes. I came home to find that all of his belongings were gone: clothes, books, toiletries. Even his reading glasses.'

'Would anyone else take them?'

'The only other person who has a key to the house is my mother-in-law, but she swears that she didn't take anything. And not long before that, I woke up to find a home video of Chloe and Ryan playing on the TV. But I didn't put the video on myself. I woke up, and it was playing.'

Balding went to comment, but Paige continued.

'Smaller things have happened, too: I'll go to sleep in my nightgown and wake up naked with my nightgown folded up inside my drawer. I'll leave the curtains open and wake up to them closed. Small things, but they add to the bigger picture in all of this.'

'I heard about what happened at the graveyard.'

'Yes, the graveyard – something happened there, too. The police officers asked me about another car being there, as though someone had followed me and watched me.'

'Paige, you drink. You drink a lot. Are you sure you didn't do these things yourself and forget? The video? Taking off your nightgown in the night? Getting rid of Ryan's things?'

He doesn't believe me. He thinks I'm insane.

'I didn't do those things, Graham. I came home and his things were gone. I woke up to the video playing – I haven't watched those films in years. I would remember getting them out again.'

'Your husband committed suicide. You're grieving. You're probably drinking more than usual, which makes you more likely to act out of character. According to the report on the graveyard incident you said you didn't remember doing it or why.'

'But these things didn't happen because of my drinking. I didn't do any of this. I wouldn't forget chucking out all of my husband's things. My drinking can't be blamed for the other car in the graveyard, can it?'

'Except for the car in the graveyard, I don't really see any other answer to what's happening. Your mother-in-law said she didn't take Ryan's belongings, and she is the only other person with a key to your house. Were there signs of breaking and entering?'

'Well no, but—'

'Paige, I'm sorry, but I reckon you're overthinking this. It sounds like you've been drinking, acting out, and then forgetting about it. I'm like that when I drink. A lot of people are.'

'Graham, I didn't do any of it. I know I didn't. I'm not mad.'

'Why would someone do those things? What's in it for them to fold up your nightgown and clear out your husband's sock drawer?'

'I don't know. That's why I called you.'

'I think you need to drink a little less. The less you drink, the more you'll remember, and the clearer everything will become.'

Paige began to doubt herself.

'Well, explain the other car in the graveyard then. I can't be blamed for that.'

'The graveyard could be a new dogging area. I've heard of odder places.'

She hadn't thought of that. 'Graham, I'm not mad.'

'I'm not saying that, Paige. I'm telling you to stop drinking.'

Balding took another sip of coffee and glanced at his watch.

'It's been ten years since Chloe was killed,' she said, hoping he would stay a little longer.

'I know. I never forget a case. Especially unsolved ones.'

She longed to ask him so many questions, but she knew he wouldn't know the answers. *Why Chloe? Why us? Why my family?* The only person who knew the answers was the person who killed her daughter.

'Will you ever revisit it? Try and find out what happened to her?'

'It has already been up for review, Paige. You know that. The decision was made to leave it be. I'm sorry. If no new leads come around within a decade, it's hard to imagine finding anything else now.'

'So cases like Chloe's are swept under the rug? How many other dead girls are under there?'

'Let's just say that Chloe isn't alone. I'm sorry, but the budget is tight and controlled from higher up – it's not my decision to make.'

Balding looked at his watch again. 'I'm sorry, I have to go.' He rested his hand on top of hers. 'Once you stop drinking, you'll realise that nothing is wrong, that all of this was just a misunderstanding.'

She couldn't say anything. In a moment she would be alone again; the thought made her bottom lip begin to quiver.

'Take care of yourself,' he said and headed for the door. As he placed the hood of his coat over his head and took hold of the door handle, he looked back at her. Pity glimmered in his eyes. He nodded farewell, and left.

I'm not mad.

A tear slid from underneath her sunglasses. She wiped it away as quickly as she could.

But what if I am?

8

The moment she returned home from the coffee shop, doubting herself and fearing insanity, she remembered the gun. Falling in the river, Ryan's possessions vanishing into thin air, the scene at her in-laws' house – she had completely forgot about the gun hidden in her house.

Paige raced up the stairs towards the office, leaving wet footprints in her wake, and paused in the doorway.

Do I want to know the truth? Haven't I gone through enough without digging up Ryan's secrets?

She stood there, watching dust dance in the path of the sunlight shining through the window, and considered shutting the door on the office for good.

I'm not mad. This could explain everything.

With a new wave of courage, she walked towards the desk, opened the drawer, and removed the false bottom.

The black handgun was waiting for her. The old phone lay beside it.

Ryan had owned a smartphone. She had never seen this phone before.

With a tentative hand, she reached down and picked up the gun. She hadn't expected it to be so heavy. It was hard and cold. She could feel her pulse in her grip on the gun.

This is too dangerous. Put it back and leave it there.

But she couldn't, not now. With the gun in one hand, she picked up the phone with the other and went downstairs. She placed the gun on the coffee table delicately, as though it were a ticking bomb. Adrenaline pulsed through her. She turned on the phone and waited. She ignored the dry puddle of sick on the carpet.

You can still take them back upstairs. You never have to know. You can move on with your life, forget all of this.

As soon as the phone turned on, she went straight to the text messages. The only messages were from an unsaved number, replying either *yes* or *no*. She searched the Sent folder. Her husband had sent about five texts to the same number. The last one read:

Meet you outside the Bird Block. Usual time?

She knew about the Bird Block. Everyone in Maidstone knew about it. It was a particular block of flats on the Tovil Estate, a block that was said to house dozens of prostitutes. Once the girls went in there, they never came back out. Drug overdoses, rough sex turned ugly, beatings, robberies and police raids. People only went to Bird Block to pay for sex or cause trouble.

The phone trembled in her hand.

Ryan wouldn't go there for sex. He was a better man than that. He could have got any willing girl to sleep with him. He wouldn't need to pay.

The sun shone through the window and reflected in the metal of the gun.

Why did you need a gun, Ryan?

She poured herself a glass of wine and returned to the sofa. She needed to calm her nerves. Before she could change her mind, she began to write a text message on the old phone to the mysterious number.

It took her over five minutes to punch out the message using the outmoded keypad.

I need to see you. Meet me outside Bird Block. Eight p.m. Important.

She read the message over and over, reluctant to send it. The person could be dangerous. This could be a huge mistake.

She pressed send and drained the wine from the glass. She leaned back on the sofa and waited for a reply.

9

The taxi pulled up outside the Bird Block and Paige instantly felt nauseous.

You can still go home. You can forget all of this.

The taxi driver had been friendly until Paige had told him where she wanted to go. They spent the drive in an awkward silence. Paige took the water bottle filled with wine from her bag and took a big gulp.

The driver turned around in his seat and faced her.

'Are you sure you want to get out here, love?'

No. Take me home. I want to go home.

She nodded unconvincingly. 'Can you wait for me?'

The driver hesitated. 'I can come back in an hour,' he said at last.

He wasn't going to stay on the Tovil Estate for an hour. His car would be picked apart and sold off in pieces in that time.

Paige looked out of the window at the Bird Block,

reluctant to leave the safety of the taxi. The brown-brick building stood five storeys high. Some windows were dark, while others were lit up, the rooms on the other side hidden by blinds or curtains. She didn't want to know what was happening in the darkness. She imagined dozens of girls lying under sweating, grunting strangers, while all they could do was dream of their next fix.

Paige paid the fare and held onto the door handle, too terrified to open it.

'You'll come back and take me home? You won't forget?'

'I'll be back.'

Paige got out of the taxi on shaking legs and watched as the taxi drove away just in time for her to close the door.

Please come back. Please don't forget me.

A streetlight flickered above her. A dog was barking. Sirens wailed in the distance. Music rumbled from a nearby house.

I shouldn't have done this. I should have stayed home.

She walked up the path towards the building and stood in the shadows by the door. Her hands were quivering as she took her cigarettes and lighter from her bag. She checked the phone: no reply. She had waited for a reply until six in the evening before she decided to head to the block of flats and wait.

Maybe the person doesn't even use that phone number anymore. This could be a complete waste of time.

Now that she was closer to the building, she could see how neglected it was. Duct tape covered cracks in the glass panel of the door; the concrete path was covered in cigarette butts and litter; a used condom lay underneath a ground floor window. Was it her imagination, or could she hear the distant sound of a woman screaming?

She hugged her coat close to her body and pulled up the hood to cover her face. As soon as she finished the cigarette she lit another, and then another. She sipped wine from the water bottle until it was gone.

What the hell am I doing? I should never have come here. I'm so stupid. I need to go home right now.

She could smell cannabis in the air. More sirens. Loud music blared from passing cars. A girl was definitely screaming.

The clock on the phone screen changed to 20:40. She had given the person over thirty minutes to appear.

Maybe I got it wrong. Maybe Ryan was paying young girls to pleasure him in the worst part of town.

She thought about calling the number.

I can still go home where it's safe. I don't have to do this.

She remembered how DI Balding had looked at her – he thought she was crazy.

She called the number and held the phone to her ear.

The dialling tone began to sound.

And then she heard the phone's ringtone from behind her.

She tried to scream but only managed muffled whimpers behind the stranger's hand as she was yanked from the darkness and through the front door of the Bird Block. She couldn't see her attacker, but she could feel a strong body behind hers and hot, laboured breaths close to her ear. An arm was wrapped around her neck in a chokehold as she was dragged up the stairs to the first floor. Paige kicked her legs wildly. Tears ran down her face, soaking the stranger's hand. As they reached the first floor, she sank her teeth into the skin. The rough hands pushed her away and down the stairs. Each blow felt like a punch as she hit her head, her back, her ankle, her wrist, her nose, before landing on the concrete of the ground floor with a thud. Hot blood trickled down her face. Pain pulsed through her in waves. She looked up to see her attacker coming down the stairs towards her.

He had dark brown skin and a gold tooth glinted from within his snarl. Tattoos covered his neck and hands, and on his face was a small black teardrop, just below his left eye.

She shrank away as he reached down and snatched her arm.

'Get up,' he spat, and dragged her back up the stairs.

She couldn't see her attacker anymore, she was dizzy and tears blurred her vision, but she could feel the anger in his tight grip and the sound of his fast breaths. He led her up through the building, leaving droplets of her blood in their wake. On the third floor, he flattened her to the wall with his face an inch from hers.

'What… what do you want?' she asked with blood on her lips.

'That's what I was going to ask you.' He put his free hand into his pocket and flashed the phone screen in her face.

The taste of blood filled her mouth. Tears ran down her cheeks. Her scalp was hot and pulsing. She had made a huge mistake.

'I'm sorry, my husband…'

'Not here.'

He snatched her wrist and led her along the hallway towards the next flight of stairs. Her shoes scuffed along the dirty floor, and her wrist burned from his grip.

'Please… please don't kill—'

'Shut up.'

I should have brought the gun. Maybe that's why Ryan had it. Maybe he needed it to protect himself whenever he met this man.

She could barely string thoughts together as she tried to think of a plan.

Kick him in the crotch and run. What if he has a knife or a gun? Should I scream? Will anybody in this block care?

They stopped on the fourth floor. A young girl, barely

able to stand, was leaning on a respectable-looking man in his fifties, dressed in a suit and tie. He immediately looked to the ground.

'You see anything tonight?' Paige's attacker asked.

'No. I didn't see anything,' replied the man, flattening himself to the wall so they could pass.

'What you doing with that old bitch?' the young girl said in a foreign accent. 'You can have me. I'm still tight. Wanna test?' she lifted up her skirt and flashed herself. Semen was slithering down her bruised thigh. She stumbled forward on her high heels and landed against Paige's attacker, who pushed her to the ground with one hand.

The man in the suit yanked the girl upright. He looked terrified. His eyes went to the blood dripping from Paige's jaw.

Paige was dragged past them and up to the fifth floor. Her heart was racing. Nervous sweat dripped down her sides.

The man opened a door on the fifth floor and shoved her into the darkness. She hit the floor hard. He slammed the door shut and turned on the light.

It was a small room with a double bed. Everything was shabby, dirty, and dated. Damp speckled the ceiling and cobwebs sat in the corners; the carpet was covered in stains. The room reeked of marijuana and stale sex. A used condom hung over the edge of the bin by her head.

The man stepped over her and headed for the table in the corner. He tossed something onto the table. She heard the spark of a lighter and saw rising smoke. He turned, sat on the edge of the bed and stared at her on the floor.

'Please, this was a mistake. I should never have come here. Just let me go. I won't say anything to anyone!'

'Why did you text me?'

Her words tumbled out of her in a nervous rush. 'My husband, Ryan, he had a phone to text you – only you. I wanted to find out what he was up to. I found the phone and a gun. He committed suicide two months ago.'

She stared at him from the floor, watching him think and smoke, never taking his eyes off her. He threw her a cigarette and a lighter. He knew she smoked. He must have been watching her for a while. She stared at the cigarette on the filthy floor, unable to understand the act of generosity. A tear dropped onto the carpet. She took the cigarette and tried to light it, but her hands were shaking too hard and wet with her own blood. The man got up, crouched over her and lit the cigarette. He sat back down and Paige leaned against the foot of the bed, taking deep drags on the shaking cigarette.

'I remember your husband. Don't see many people like him round here.'

Paige wiped her cheeks of blood and tears and focused on the man's deep, slow voice.

'Didn't know he killed himself, neither.' He took a drag on the cigarette and studied her. 'You shouldn't have come here.'

'Please…' she begged without anything left to say. Her life was in his hands.

'I'm not a nice man. I kill. I kill to live.'

'You're… a hitman?'

He nodded his head once. 'And other things. Gets you paranoid, this job. You kill people, others come lookin'.'

'I won't tell anyone about what you do, I swear. I only came to find out why my husband had a gun.'

'Well he didn't come to me for a chat. You figure it out.'

'Why? Who would he want dead so badly?'

'Confidential, innit. Ain't about to break my word to a dead man. I ain't no snitch.'

'Did you do it? Did you kill whoever he wanted dead?'

He took a drag on his cigarette. 'He called it off night before. Asked for a gun instead. Paid a lot for it, too.'

If Paige hadn't been so terrified, she would have begged him to tell her. The fear of rape sat in the back of her mind. She eyed the condom on the edge of the bin.

'I won't contact you again. I'll give you the phone. Here.' She slid the phone across the stained carpet.

'Do you know how stupid you are coming here?'

'I'm sorry… I just… I had to know what he was up to.'

'Your man bought a gun from me, lady. Whatever

he was mixed up in ain't worth your time, or your life. Prob'ly wanted to kill the man himself.'

What man? Who would Ryan want to kill?

'You can go.'

She stared at him in disbelief.

'You don't wanna stay here, lady, trust me. Get up and fuck off.'

Paige scrambled to her feet, the cigarette still burning between her fingers. She swung the door open and sprinted down the hallway for the stairs, following the trail of her own blood.

10

Paige woke up on the sofa to a ferocious headache. The room was dark, but daylight framed the curtains. Her scalp was burning, as though clumps of hair and skin had been ripped from the bone. The palms of her hands felt tender and hot, and her whole body ached.

The hitman.

She took a couple of codeine tablets and waited for the pain to ease. It was as though her wounds had their own pulses, all of them screaming to be soothed.

Paige went upstairs and showered, standing in a crimson pool as blood circled the drain by her feet. The shower gel stung her grazed palms.

Once dry, she stood in front of the full-length mirror in her bedroom and let the towel fall to the floor. Cuts and bruises covered her pale skin, like milk in a dirty glass. Her body was a bundle of contradictions wrapped in skin: she was too skinny in some areas, which was evident from her protruding ribs and collarbones, but plump in others, like the tyre of fat that was forming around her hips and stomach from drinking. In some lights she looked youthful: she had firm breasts that had not yet sagged; but in other lights her body revealed its age, as shown by the crow's feet that had begun to form at the corners of her yellowing eyes. The faded scar from her caesarean smiled at her in the mirror. She ran a finger along it, feeling its ridges and bumps, and promised herself not to cry. Chloe had died and left nothing but scars.

She studied her reflection: scraped hands and knees, bruises all over her body from the fall down the stairs, and a throbbing wound on her scalp that was hot to the touch. Her arm was covered in bruises from the hitman's fingers digging into her skin.

Paige sat on the bed as she slipped on her underwear and hooked her bra in place. She looked at the photo frame on her side of the bed.

It was a photo of the three of them together: Ryan, Chloe, and her. But Ryan's face was no longer there – it had been cut out.

Paige snatched the frame from the bedside table and examined it.

I didn't do this.

She threw on her dressing gown and began to check

every photo frame in the house: he had been cut out of all of them.

This can't be happening. I know I didn't do this. I'm not crazy.

She knelt before the bookshelf in the living room and grabbed the photo albums from the bottom shelf. She flicked open the first album and raced through the pages. Ryan's face had been removed from the photos: Ryan holding Chloe in the hospital after her birth, Ryan pushing Chloe on her first bike, their first family vacation abroad, birthdays, Christmases. He had been erased from every picture they had.

'I'm not mad,' she whispered over and over as tears fell onto the pages.

Paige frantically searched every album, flicking the pages faster and faster, seeing nothing but holes where Ryan's face should have been.

Surrounded by tarnished photo albums, she sobbed into her grazed hands.

What is happening to me?

A photo from Chloe's first birthday looked up at her from an open album. Chloe's eyes were glowing from the lit candles, Paige was smiling and genuinely happy, sitting beside a man without a face.

How will I remember what he looks like?

However angry she was at Ryan, she wouldn't do this – she wouldn't go this far, however much she drank. She grabbed her mobile and called DI Graham Balding.

'Balding,' he said.

'Graham, it's Paige Dawson.'

'Oh, hi,' he said, sounding distracted. 'Everything all right?'

'No, it isn't. Someone has come into my house and cut Ryan's face out of all our photographs.' She waited eagerly for his response, for him to finally believe her.

'You drove into your husband's gravestone the other night, Paige. It wouldn't surprise me if you did this too. I told you – you need to stop drinking.'

'I didn't do this, I swear…'

'Are there signs of breaking and entering?'

'No, but…'

'Are you still drinking?'

'This isn't happening because of my damn drinking!'

'Paige, go to therapy and put down the bottle, and then these things will stop. Trust me.'

'Graham, I didn't do this! I promise you, I didn't!'

'Who else could have done it?'

'That's why I'm calling you, I don't know!'

'You're angry with your husband for committing suicide. You're so angry that you drove into his gravestone. Now you've done this. I'm sorry Paige, but I can't have you calling me every time you drink too much and screw up. I have real cases to solve.'

'Well, I hope you don't have any missing girls relying on you. Your track record isn't too good, is it?'

She sat on the floor, staring at her faceless husband as the dialling tone rang in her ear.

11

Paige was drunk when the doorbell rang. She opened the door to find Greta on the other side. Without a word, Paige went back to the sofa and Greta came inside.

The destroyed photo albums lay strewn across the carpet. An empty wine bottle sat on the coffee table beside another half-full bottle and a freshly poured glass. Greta stared at the mess.

'I didn't do it,' Paige said, before taking a gulp of wine. 'You won't believe me. No one else does.'

Greta stared at her, lost for words.

'I thought you hated me,' Paige said.

'I could never hate you.'

'I'd hate me.'

Greta took the empty bottle of wine and went into the kitchen. Paige heard the bottle fall into the bin and a cupboard open and close. Greta came back into the living room with a wine glass and filled it with wine from the bottle on the table. She sat on the opposite sofa and took a sip. Paige hadn't seen her drink before.

'I'm not going to hold what happened against you. You're a broken woman, Paige. You have poor judgement, a skewed outlook on the world, but you're not malicious. I know that.' She took another sip. 'I've been hard on you and I'm sorry. I shouldn't scold you for grieving differently from me.'

Greta looked down at the photo albums and sighed.

She thinks I'm mad, just like everybody else.

'With Chloe and Ryan gone, there is nothing to keep our bond but memories. I don't want to lose you from this family. You might not be blood, but you've been a part of our lives for twenty years. I'm not going to lose you now.'

'Does Richard think that, too?'

'Yes.'

'I doubt that, after what I did.'

'We've talked about it. We all grieve differently, he sees that now.'

They sat in silence for a moment, sipping at wine in the house full of memories.

'Do you still want to be a part of this family?'

'Yes.'

'I'm glad.'

'You can have your key back.'

It sat among the mess on the coffee table. Greta picked it up.

'Thank you.'

Greta looked at the wine in her glass.

'Are you eating?'

Paige tried to remember the last time she ate. Had it really been the day she returned from the police station? She had to have eaten since then.

'I'll make you something.'

Paige looked at her watch.

'I have to go out soon.'

Criticism sat at the tip of Greta's tongue, but she kept it locked behind clenched teeth.

Yes, I'm leaving the house drunk.

'I'll make something for you – you can eat it when you get home.'

'Okay.'

Paige drank the rest of her wine and stood unsteadily; Greta stood, too. Neither knew what they should do. Hug? Kiss?

Paige went to the door, slipped into her shoes, and put her bag over her shoulder.

'See you soon.'

'Yes,' Greta said.

Paige shut the door.

*　　*　　*

Paige read the posters on the wall, bent over Dr Abdullah's desk. She tried to ignore his beast-like grunts and the feel of him inside of her. She read the posters and wondered how much longer it would take for him to climax.

His sweaty hands grasped her waist. If only he could do it without holding her.

Stop thinking of his hands. Think of the posters. Look at them, nothing else.

A Samaritans poster was stuck to the wall, with the headline: 'Don't face depression alone: talk to someone.'

If only it were as simple as that, she thought as she jolted with the doctor's thrusts.

She had never seen her sexual relationship with the doctor as abusive, but instead viewed it as two consumers trading with each other: he wanted sex; she wanted pills. But the more she visited Dr Abdullah, and the more she got on her knees and tasted him in her mouth, she realised that he knew exactly how she felt about their encounters. He wasn't stupid. He knew that she hated every minute of it. If he tried to kiss her, she turned her head away. When he climaxed in her mouth, she spat it out as though it were toxic. The way she looked at him must have shown how she felt about him. Dr Abdullah had the nerve to look into her eyes, see a damaged, lost woman, and unzip his flies.

Posters. Look at the posters. Stop thinking about him.

Dr Abdullah's grunts got louder and deeper. If she

hadn't been so disgusted with him and with herself, Paige would have laughed. She winced when his grip on her waist tightened.

Oh good. It's nearly over now.

He thrust one final time, hard and deep, and stayed there for a moment, quivering against her. Paige waited, staring lifelessly at the wall, at the posters, until he released her.

They dressed in silence, filled with shame and embarrassment. Once dressed, the doctor sat in his desk chair.

'The pills,' she said.

He nodded silently, still out of breath, and retrieved the packets from the top drawer of his desk. She took them from him and turned to head for the door.

'Wait. I need to speak with you.'

She faced him, and remained standing even when he signalled for her to sit down. He sighed, took off his glasses and rubbed his eyes.

'That was the last time.'

The words hit her like fists.

'What?'

'I can't risk my whole career for…' he cleared his throat, considering his words. 'You. I can't keep doing this with you.'

She couldn't say anything. All she could do was stare at him through building tears. *I need my pills.*

'My colleagues are beginning to notice the missing stock. A pack here and there was manageable, but now you're taking so much more and I can't cover my tracks. If this continues, there will be an investigation into the missing stock. I can't lose my job, my licence, my family for… you.'

'You mean sex. You aren't doing this for *me* – we're not lovers – you're doing it to get your end away. Stop trying to be poetic.'

'You know what I mean. And you know, deep down, that this is wrong.'

'I'll tell them.'

'Pardon?'

'I'll tell them that you were stealing pills to give to me in exchange for sex.'

'I'm trying to do the right thing, Paige.'

'I need my damn pills! Don't do this to me.'

'I'm sorry.'

'Screw your apology. I want my pills!'

'You won't be getting any extras from me. You won't tell, I know you won't.'

'And why won't I? What have I got to lose?'

'The last bit of self-respect you have left.'

She could feel warm tears on her face, but she was too angry to wipe them away. Her hands balled up into furious fists by her sides.

'Could you really go out there and tell my colleagues

what you've been doing? Bending over this desk, getting down on your knees? I don't think your dignity can take another battering, do you?'

When the desk lamp hit his head the bulb shattered. His glasses fell from his face and blood began to trickle from a cut above his brow. He barely had time to cover his face before she began hitting him with her fists. Every punch symbolised each time he had used her body as a self-gratifying tool, for knowing that she longed for it end as quickly as possible, and doing it anyway. After a few blows, he snatched one wrist, and then the other, and looked at her with utter contempt.

'Get out of here, you whore!'

She spat in his face and ran out the door as the saliva slithered down his cheek.

Everyone in the waiting room stared at her: the deranged woman stumbling to the door with tears shimmering on her face. She stormed out of the GP surgery and sobbed into her hands.

12

Paige woke up to the memory of her altercation with the doctor. She couldn't seem to leave her bed, or even lift the duvet from over her face. Reality was waiting for her, but she longed for it to leave her be.

Her mouth was dry and sticky, and her head was pounding. She couldn't remember the last time she woke up without a hangover, or woke up in her bed and not the sofa.

She hadn't washed the bed sheets since Ryan last slept in them. She burrowed her face into the sheets, inhaled him, and longed for him to be back in her life, by her side, so she didn't have to keep waking up alone.

What sort of forty-two-year-old woman has sex in exchange for drugs, with a man who repulses her?

Contempt washed over her like bleach as she remembered the act. She felt filthy and disgusted with herself. She resented every breath she took.

Her hand crept out from under the duvet and patted the bedside table, feeling for her tablets. Her fingertips felt an empty tray – she had taken them all.

She got up and groaned. Even that made her feel nauseous.

The room reeked of alcohol and cigarette smoke. She coughed hard and heard phlegm loosen in her lungs as she headed for the bathroom to pee. Blood swam in her urine beneath her. She flushed it away.

Why had she agreed to the arrangement with him? Why did she let men treat her like that? Like an object to be used? It was as though the acceptance of abuse was hardwired into her brain. The doctor hadn't forced her, she had given herself to him – he simply took what was being offered. Instead, she had been the abuser: by giving herself to him, by not respecting her body and her worth, she had violated herself.

She had no idea when the cycle of recklessness began, but she knew that it had to stop. That kind of encounter wasn't just a violation of her body, but of her mind. It plagued her mind like a poison, as though the physical act were a venomous bite. The bite hurt, but it ended – it was the venom that seeped into her body until it had polluted every single part of her. It changed everything she knew. Being touched by another person's hand was like being scorched with a branding iron.

As she left the bathroom for the stairs, she stopped in her tracks. Chloe's bedroom door had been left ajar.

Did I go in there last night?

She couldn't remember, and couldn't escape the feeling that something was wrong.

She pushed the door open.

The room didn't smell like her daughter anymore. It smelt of fresh air, laundry detergent, and furniture polish. The carpet had been vacuumed. Paige stepped inside.

The bed sheets had been stripped and replaced with a clean set. The window was open to let cold air enter the room and Chloe's scent escape. Every surface had been polished; objects had been tidied away; the photos and posters had been ripped from the walls; everything had changed. It wasn't Chloe's room anymore.

Paige knelt down in front of the bed and pressed the duvet to her wet cheeks. She inhaled, but smelt nothing of her, only detergent. It was as though in destroying Chloe's memory, in ridding her of her final connection to Chloe, her daughter had been killed all over again. She sobbed into the duvet until she heard the front door open.

Greta did this.

She ran out of the room and down the stairs. Greta was talking up to her, until Paige slammed her into the front door.

'*How could you do that!*'

'What did I do?'

'*You destroyed it! You destroyed everything!*'

'You're mad! You really have gone mad!'

'*Why did you do it? Why did you have to take her away from me.*' Paige's face was inches from Greta's, her saliva spraying onto her skin. She pulled Greta from the door and shoved her against it again. '*I hate you! You're dead to me!*'

She yanked Greta from the door by her blouse and threw the door open.

Greta stood in the living room, sobbing, with a rip in her blouse that revealed her vest and lily-white skin.

'GET OUT!'

Paige lunged forward, snatched Greta, dragged her to the door and shoved her out of the house. She picked up Greta's bag from the carpet and threw it out of the door. Her belongings scattered on the ground.

Paige slammed the door shut, fell against it, and sobbed as she slid to the floor. She looked up the stairs from where she sat, staring at the door to Ryan's office.

If only he hadn't died. None of this would have happened.

She had lost nearly everyone in her life: her daughter, her husband, her in-laws and her doctor – and with him, her pills. All she had was her lonely life and her empty house filled with ghosts of the past.

A thought came to her.

The gun.

She had put it back in Ryan's desk. She raced up the stairs, bounded into the office and threw open the drawer.

The gun was gone.

13

Paige had only turned her back for a minute and Chloe had vanished. She found her sitting on the floor in the toy section in front of a large purple bear with love hearts for eyes.

'I'll buy it for you, darling, but only if you don't run off again.'

She took Chloe's hand and led her to the checkout counter. The young retail assistant stifled a yawn and scanned the price tag without even looking at them.

'Nineteen pounds ninety-nine.'

'For a bear?'

'That's what it says.'

Wise arse.

Paige searched for her purse inside her handbag. When she found it and tried to pull out her debit card, change scattered all over the floor.

'Chloe, pick them up for me, would you?'

Chloe didn't move at first, just continued to stare up at Paige, almost as though she was frightened of her.

She doesn't like it when I drink.

'Please, Chloe, help Mummy.'

Paige paid for the bear as Chloe slowly picked up the coins. She opened her handbag and told Chloe to put the coins inside. She would sort it all out later when they got home.

With the bear tucked under Chloe's arm they continued to walk around the store. Paige couldn't remember why they were there. It hadn't been for the bear or the shoes.

'We could get a tie for Daddy,' Paige said. 'That might be nice. What colour do you think he would like?'

Chloe didn't say anything; she was too distracted by her new bear.

'I think red, although he loves blue,' she went on.

They were halfway up the escalator when they heard a commotion from below.

'STOP! STOP HER!'

The words echoed around the department store. Paige looked down the escalator to see all of the other shoppers looking up her. Paige turned around and looked up, trying to see who they were looking at, and saw the shoppers above her peering down at her too.

Me. They're all looking at me.

Paige stared down again to see the shoppers on the escalator stand aside for a screaming woman who was running up the steps towards her. Not far behind her was a security guard.

'I haven't stolen anything,' Paige said. 'I paid for the bear, I have the receipt in my bag.'

The woman smacked Paige in the face with a clenched fist, just as they reached the top of the escalator. Paige fell on her back, pulling Chloe down with her.

'Get off her!' the woman yelled. 'Let go of my daughter!'

The woman leaped forward and grabbed Chloe as the security guard snatched Paige by the hood of her coat and yanked her to her feet.

'Get off Chloe! She's mine! That's my girl! That's my daughter!'

Everyone was staring at her. The woman was taking Chloe away.

'She's mine!' Paige screamed, trying to rush to her daughter, but the guard held her back.

Chloe was hugging the woman who was taking her away, sobbing into her neck.

And then Paige saw the truth: the little girl wasn't Chloe.

She looked like Chloe: red hair, blue eyes, freckles on milky white skin – but she wasn't Paige's daughter.

'Come with me,' the guard said. 'Don't make this difficult.'

'I'm sorry,' Paige said, slurring her words and stumbling as he dragged her back towards the escalator.

'Sorry for trying to snatch a kid?'

'I thought she was my daughter.'

'You can't be that drunk, love.'

They stepped onto the escalator and took the slow journey down. There was a deafening silence as every shopper stared at Paige and the security guard, their eyes boring into her. She felt hot and disorientated, burning up beneath her coat. Her whole body was quivering. When they reached the ground floor, she vomited. The bloody bile splashed on the floor. Onlookers grimaced.

The guard spoke into his radio, documenting the act.

'I'm sorry,' she said again, bile dripping from her bottom lip. 'This was a mistake. I was confused.'

'Save it for the police, lady.'

Suddenly she realised how serious it was. This wasn't just a misunderstanding – she was about to be in trouble with the police again, but this time it was for taking a child who wasn't hers.

The guard dragged her through aisles as shoppers looked on. Mothers held their children closer, and men looked at her as though she was deranged.

Eventually, the guard led her through a doorway and into a small office, and then took her through to an even smaller, windowless room with a bench. She sat down and the door slammed shut behind her.

What the hell have I done?

14

'Stop apologising, Paige. It's getting really old.'

Maxim was really upset this time, gripping onto the steering wheel as though it were her neck. He had collected her from police custody for the second time. Maxim had rushed to the department store where the police had questioned her in the small office for over two hours. With Maxim's help, the police didn't see her as a perverted child-snatcher, but a deranged woman who had thought she'd found her dead daughter in the toy section. Somehow she managed to walk away without cuffs on her wrists.

The skin on her cheeks itched from the old, dried tears. The bombardment of questions had sobered her, and the adrenaline finally began to dissipate; all she wanted to do now was go to sleep and never wake up.

'What were you *thinking?*'

'I wasn't. I thought... I thought the girl was... For

some reason I believed Chloe wasn't…' She stopped talking to fight back the oncoming tears.

'I can't keep getting you out of these situations. You're going to end up in prison, Paige!'

'I know. I'm going to change, I promise.'

'When? You've been doing this for the last ten years.'

'Now – I promise.'

'You have to, before you wind up dead. You're running yourself into an early grave, Paige, and I can't witness it anymore.'

'I'm sorry.'

Maxim sighed as he pulled up to the kerb outside Paige's house. They both sat in silence.

'I love you so much, Paige, but I can't keep doing this with you. I can't sleep at night for worrying that you're lying dead somewhere, or you're too drunk to remember that you left the stove on, or you've overdosed on those damn tablets you take. The way I'm heading, I'll be having a heart attack just like Dad had.'

Guilt stabbed at her chest like a knife.

'I'm going to change, Maxim, I promise. I'm going to go to sleep when I get in – and when I wake up, I'm going to be a new woman.'

He pulled her into him and hugged her tight. His facial hair scratched her forehead.

'I love you,' he said.

'Love you, too,' she replied, feeling uncomfortable inside a man's arms.

'I think you should stay with me. You can't be trusted to live on your own.'

'I'm fine Maxim, please. I need to do this on my own.'

She shut the car door and headed inside.

The moment she got inside, she poured herself a glass of wine to calm her nerves and swallowed down two pills. She drained the glass and headed upstairs. She was going to go to sleep and wake up to a new day, a fresh start, a better Paige.

* * *

Paige woke up to the smell of smoke, but it wasn't the smoke she was used to. This smoke was dark and thick, and scratched her throat as though she had swallowed razor blades. An alarm wailed from downstairs.

She sat up and tried to heave the smoke from her lungs, but coughing only seemed to make it worse. The room was dark and clouded with the toxic black smoke; every time she coughed it up, she drew more in, as though she were drowning in it. She crawled out of bed, staggered through the black fog to the window and threw it open, revealing the night sky and the lights turning on in the windows of the houses across the street. She breathed in the clean air as smoke billowed out around her. She coughed so hard that she retched, spewing bile down to the ground below.

Neighbours began to emerge from their houses in dressing gowns and slippers, and congregated outside the burning house. Panic swept through them. Voices shouted up to her. Children were crying.

The floor beneath her bare feet was hot – so hot she could barely stand on it. She looked back into the room, trying to see if there were flames, but the smoke stung her eyes like sharp needles. She snapped her head back as her eyes began to stream.

I have to jump.

Her head felt heavy as the carbon dioxide began to fill her body.

If I don't jump I'll burn alive.

The faint sound of sirens called in the distance, but they wouldn't arrive in time to save her. If she wanted to live, she had to jump.

She lifted one shaking leg over the windowsill, and then the other, and stared down at the ground that seemed so far away.

'I can't do it!' she cried out to the onlookers.

A woman screamed. People watched from behind twitching curtains. People were yelling out to her. The smoke was getting thicker and her head was getting lighter.

The next thing she knew she was falling. Her body slammed to the ground with such a jolt that she heard a bone snap. She looked up at the window, at the black smoke gushing out and rising into the sky.

Neighbours rushed around her, just as everything went dark.

15

Her home burned to the ground, and all of her belongings and memories went up in smoke, yet her first thought had been: *all of my pills are gone. Sleeping with Dr Abdullah has been for nothing.*

Sitting on Maxim's sofa with a mug of tea in one hand and a cast fixed to the other, Paige tried to digest the fact that everything of Chloe's, of Ryan's, of hers, was now crumbling ash or charred black.

It had been her fault. The firefighters suspected that the fire had started from a cigarette. She couldn't even remember smoking when she got home.

The doctor said that nearly dying in the fire had saved her life. If she hadn't been admitted to hospital, she may not have discovered she had alcoholic hepatitis until it was too late. The blood in her urine and vomit, the back pain, the confusion – they were all side effects of her failing liver. She had been slowly killing herself for the last ten years. Deep down, she had known that all along.

She had been so sure that she wasn't to blame for cutting Ryan from the photos or dumping his belongings, but mistaking a young girl for her dead daughter had been her undoing – she couldn't blame that on someone else.

Did someone take the gun? Or had it never existed in the first place? Just how sick am I?

The occurrences weren't happening *to* her, they were *because* of her, and she had been lucky to leave with her life. Her only injuries were a broken wrist, bruised ribs, a sprained ankle, and a mild concussion.

Paige was taking chlordiazepoxide to ease her withdrawal symptoms as she stopped drinking alcohol, and smaller doses of the diazepam and codeine that her body had come to depend on. She hadn't been given a choice; the decision had been made for her: no more alcohol or drugs.

Maxim didn't drink much, but that didn't stop Paige from searching his house. There were two places she hadn't checked yet: a bedroom upstairs and the cupboard under the stairs. Both were locked. She decided to hunt for the keys the moment he left the house on another errand.

She was glad to be out of the hospital. It wasn't just the needles and clinical smell she was glad to be free of, but the frenzied media presence that plagued the hospital like a swarm of wasps.

A two-year-old boy had been left outside the hospital, severely ill with pneumonia and close to death. A photo of him had been leaked to the press, prompting reporters and camera crews – who were longing to unearth the secret of the mystery boy without a family – to build a base outside the building. The hospital was on lockdown, with policemen surrounding the paediatric ward and badgering every visitor who attempted to enter the walls of the hospital. Paige hadn't noticed at first, she was too spaced out from the medication, but during her second night, she heard the commotion outside, saw the flashes of cameras at the windows, and overheard the nurses whispering about the boy while at their station. When Paige had left the hospital to meet Maxim in the car park, she saw the boy's green, helpless eyes staring out from every newspaper stand, and thought to herself, *at least my life isn't that bad.*

When the front door opened, Paige expected to see Maxim, but instead, she saw her father, his face filled with worry. He approached her without a word and held her tight.

'I'm safe, Dad.'

'For how long?'

'I'm changing. I promise. I haven't had a drink in nearly four days and I'm slowly coming off the pills.'

He pulled away from her and then looked into her eyes, cupping her face in his hands.

'You have no idea how much I love you, do you?'

Tears filled his eyes, begging to fall. Paige had only seen her father cry once, and that was at her mother's funeral.

He shook his head, as though angry at the tears, and sat next to her on the sofa.

'I got you cigarettes, in case Maxim is too proud to buy them.'

He took the packet out of his jacket pocket and put it on her lap.

'Wow, a dig at Maxim. I never thought I'd see the day.'

'He's a vicar. Vicars can't be seen buying twenty superkings.'

They smiled knowingly at each other.

'I bought you some bits. I wasn't sure what you might need.' He handed her the plastic bag. Inside were underwear and a bra, a toothbrush and toothpaste, sanitary towels and a hairbrush. A cheap pair of flat pumps rested at the bottom. A couple of blouses and supermarket-brand jeans were folded in together. She could see from the labels that they weren't her size.

'Thank you, Dad.'

'If you need anything else, let me know and I'll pop out and get it.'

'Dad, I haven't said this enough, so I'm going to keep

saying it until you're sick of hearing it: I'm so sorry for what I've put you through. I've been so selfish, only thinking of my own pain when I was causing other people grief.'

Her dad took her hand and squeezed it tight.

'Just get better, that's all I want. No apologies needed – I'll be happy with a peaceful night's sleep.'

'You'll get it. Especially now I'm staying here with Maxim. He can keep an eye on me and stop me from relapsing.'

'Are you sure you don't want to stay with me?'

'Dad, you have a liquor cabinet. I'd prise open any lock you put on it and drink the place dry. At least here there isn't any temptation. Besides, you don't have any room for me.'

'I just worry that… being here with Maxim…'

'You're worried that I'm living in the house that overlooks the graves of my husband and daughter.'

He hesitated, scanning her face, and nodded.

'If anything, I feel better knowing that they are so close. I've lost everything they had, we had. Now, all I have are memories and their graves. I want to be close to them.'

'I understand. But if you change your mind…'

The front door opened and Maxim entered. His cheeks were red from the chilly autumn air, and orange and red leaves followed him into the house.

'Dad,' he said. 'How're you?'

'Fine, son. Just checking in on the patient.'

'Don't worry, I'll nurse her back to health.'

He took the shopping bags into the kitchen and out of sight.

Her dad leaned in, holding her hand again, and gave it a squeeze.

'Remember,' he said, quietly. 'You can always come and stay with me.'

Maxim entered the room. 'Anyone for tea?'

'I'm going to go,' their father said, as he stood up. 'I'll come round in a few days.'

'Yeah?' Maxim replied.

'Yeah. Maybe we could have dinner.'

'That'd be nice,' Paige said.

'I guess so,' Maxim said. 'Paige, I was hoping you'd come with me to the church today.'

Oh great.

'I'd love to.'

'Brilliant. You'd best get ready.' He turned to their father. 'Good seeing you, Dad.' Maxim walked him to the door.

Their father gave Paige a wave before he left the house.

'I don't have anything to wear to the service. I only have this.' She looked down at the tracksuit that Maxim had lent her. 'Dad bought me some clothes, but they aren't my size either.'

'We probably don't have time to go shopping, but I have a long coat you could wear. What's in the bags?'

'The stuff that Dad brought over. The shoes and tights will work.'

'You can wear them with the coat until we go shopping.'

She smiled politely, as he wandered upstairs to get the coat. She suddenly felt like she was a child again, being offered to be taken places, sheltered, as though she were incapable of following her own lead. She didn't have a home of her own, a car, money, or belongings. Perhaps she needed to be guided until she could be trusted.

'Here,' Maxim said, coming down with the black coat.

Paige got up and took the coat from him, checking it over.

'Thanks.'

'You've probably got time to freshen up. Forty-five minutes, all right? I can meet you over at the church.'

'Okay.'

'I'm really glad to have you here, Pudge.' He seemed genuinely happy, and his green eyes had a brightness in them that she hadn't seen in a while. He must have been lonely, too. 'It's like we're kids again.'

*   *   *

The bathroom was freezing. Even under the hot water, the cold air bit at her wet skin. She kept the showerhead low and her plaster cast high, away from the spray. The old windows allowed a cold draft to seep into the small house; the panes shivered in their frames.

Paige got out of the shower, and dried herself down as her teeth chattered. She quickly wrapped herself in Maxim's dressing gown, which had been hanging on the back of the bathroom door, and wrapped her wet hair in a towel.

Back in the bedroom she had been told to call her own, she tried on the clothes her father had bought for her. They looked awful. She looked down at the black coat, the pair of tights, the baggy knickers, and the basic black pumps that waited for her on the bed. Paige regretted agreeing to go to the church. She would freeze.

After she had brushed her hair to let it air-dry into natural waves, she put on the underwear and tights that her father had picked out for her and tried on the coat, which was cut low and revealed too much of her chest. She sneaked into Maxim's bedroom to look for a scarf to cover her cleavage.

His room was basic and bland: a double bed with a black metal frame, a cross nailed on the wall above it, two bedside tables – one used, one not; a Bible rested on the pine chest of drawers next to the small wardrobe. She looked in the drawers and found a bright red scarf. She wrapped it around her neck and returned to her room.

'It'll have to do,' she told her reflection, and slipped her feet into the small pumps that crammed her toes together. Maxim's scarf itched against her skin, but she preferred to wear it than flash her breasts at his congregation.

She stepped out into the beautiful autumnal day. Yellow, orange, and red leaves fell from the trees surrounding the house, littering the green lawn and the pathway leading to the church. The beauty didn't escape her and, despite having lost everything, she smiled as she breathed in the fresh air and felt her cheeks flush red.

Walking down the path to the church, she wondered if this was exactly what she needed: an escape from everything she knew. Here, she was away from the house and all of the memories that had been trapped inside it and had kept her in the past. She was away from the sofa she used to drink on, and the bath where Ryan had ended his life, and where Chloe's room had only been a wall away. Staying in Maxim's house meant she had fewer reminders of her past.

Before entering the church, she walked through the graveyard, listening to the gravel crunch underfoot, trying to ignore the pain in her ankle.

She stood before their graves: Chloe and Ryan, side by side. She might be alone, but they weren't. There may be only a part of Chloe beneath the earth, but it was enough. At least a part of her was at rest, next to her father. Paige looked at Ryan's crushed gravestone, and began to pick up the rubble. She found pieces of his name etched into bits of the broken stone, and managed to line up the rocks with the letters to read his name.

'Ryan... I forgive you.'

She walked towards the church feeling lighter, with a sense of clarity she hadn't felt in years. She was free from alcohol, free from pills, feeling less grief than she had felt in a long, long time. The pain was still there, as it always would be, but for the first time, she felt like might survive it.

*   *   *

Paige stood next to Maxim at the door to the church as he greeted his congregation. He smiled and shook hands, while she handed out the hymn booklets. There weren't many people – only ten or so, all over the age of forty. Paige stood awkwardly and smiled at the strangers while sweating from the thick, itchy scarf around her neck. She longed to take it off, but was afraid of revealing the bare skin beneath.

Just then, Dr Abdullah walked towards them, his arm linked with that of a woman of his own age and ethnicity. Paige dropped the hymnbooks. Dr Abdullah's eyes met Paige's: they were both terrified; the woman and Maxim looked between them in confusion.

'Are you all right?' Maxim asked.

'I'm fine, just clumsy.'

She bent at her knees to pick them up, and saw the doctor's companion do the same, She gave Paige a kind smile.

Don't smile at me. You should hate me.

'Thanks,' she said, as she noticed the ring on the woman's finger.

'No problem,' Mrs Abdullah said, keeping two books for her and the doctor. He refused to look at Paige, as though another glance would give them away.

Paige straightened her hair and adjusted the hem of the coat, suddenly feeling exposed.

'Do you know the doctor?' Maxim asked when they were alone again.

'He's my GP.'

'Do you always react that way when you see people you know?'

'No, not always.'

When everyone was seated, Maxim made his way to the pulpit and began the service. Paige sat on the back pew and allowed herself to take off the scarf before she began to drip with sweat, wondering how long it would take until the service was over and she could get away from the doctor. His wife was beautiful, with long dark hair, hazel eyes, youthful skin – and a warm smile that Paige felt unworthy of. They were sitting five rows in front of her, and every so often the doctor would glance back to check she was still there. Paige could see the cut on his head had scabbed over and was surrounded by a purple bruise.

Dressed in just the coat and tights, Paige couldn't help but feel like a whore again, especially under the doctor's glare. Only an hour before she had been walking towards the church feeling uplifted, free from her previous burdens, but being near the doctor brought back shame. She felt judged and dirty. She longed to get back into the cold shower and scrub her skin until she felt clean again.

While Maxim delivered his sermon, he frequently looked at Paige with a smile.

At least my presence makes him happy, she thought, crossing her legs and pulling down the hem of the coat again. The doctor glanced at her.

I need to get out of here. I need a drink. I need something.

She looked at the side door leading further into the church, and wondered if she would be able find the communion wine.

No. You're doing this. You're staying sober.

The doctor glanced back at her again, and this time his wife noticed. She followed his gaze and turned to look at Paige. With that one look, Paige watched the woman learn about the relationship between her and the doctor, about what they had done. His wife's eyes glazed over with a sheen of tears.

Paige grabbed the scarf and headed for the door, and practically ran through the graveyard, longing to get away from the scrutiny. The scarf got stuck under her foot and she fell on the gravel, twisting her bad ankle, scraping her knees and laddering the tights. Her broken wrist ached from the jolt. Her free hand was bleeding. When she looked up, she saw her husband's grave.

'So you're judging me, too?'

She picked herself up and limped back to Maxim's cottage, longing to be alone, to take some of her tablets, and to forget the shame and the pain that seemed to stalk her every move.

16

Paige sat down at the dining table and took a sip of water, wishing it were wine. Dressed in Maxim's tracksuit again, her knees felt hot and sore from the fall in the graveyard. Her injured wrist still ached and her ankle was swollen. A candle flickered in the centre of the table; the flame gleamed in the cutlery that was set on the table for the two of them. Maxim was in the kitchen serving up.

He emerged with two plates of pasta in a creamy sauce, easy to eat with a fork in one hand.

'Looks great.'

'Well, you haven't eaten it yet,' he replied, and sat opposite her.

'I've been living off your dinners for a while now. I'm not looking forward to the day when I have to cook for myself again.'

'Stay here, and I'd be happy to cook for you every night.' He raised his glass of water. 'Cheers.'

Paige raised her own and they each took a sip before tucking in.

'Do you ever get lonely, Maxim? Living on your own?'

'I'm not alone,' he said. He put a forkful of pasta into his mouth and chewed. 'I have God.'

'No one else? No friend that sometimes stays?'

'I don't have a girlfriend,' he replied.

'Why not? It's not as if you aren't attractive.'

'I have everything I want. Well, almost everything. I don't feel the need for a girlfriend.'

'Surely even vicars are allowed a sex life?'

'Who says I don't have a sex life?' he raised one eyebrow and smirked.

'Touché,' she said and laughed.

They sat in silence for a few moments.

'What was all that about with the doctor today?'

'What do you mean?' she asked.

'You both looked as though you were staring at corpses.'

'I think he feels guilty about Ryan's death, you know? He prescribed him antidepressants, but clearly they weren't enough.'

'Why would that shock you enough to drop the hymnbooks?'

'I'm still getting used to this,' She raised her cast. 'I keep thinking I have the use of both hands.'

He frowned at his plate. 'Did you sleep with him?'

'Excuse me?' She looked at her brother with dismay.

'You're my little sister. I don't want you going with men like that. You're better than that.'

'What I do is none of your business.'

'Why do we have to argue every time we're together?'

'Because you pry too much.'

'I'm sorry,' he said. 'I'll work on it.'

They ate and tried to ignore the tension swelling between them. Paige longed to sip at a glass of white wine. The dinner seemed odd without it.

'You know that was his wife he came to the church with today?'

'Maxim, I really don't want to talk about it.'

'Perhaps you should think of her before you meet with him again.'

She dropped the fork onto the plate. Maxim jumped.

'If you're going to make me feel like shit, I'll go and stay with Dad.'

'You're better off here.'

'Right now, I'm not so sure.'

'I'm sorry, all right? It's because I care for you. I don't like the thought of you being with him.'

'Well, don't think about it. And you can do that by not talking about it.'

They finished their dinner in awkward silence. Paige imagined packing a bag and going to her father's, when she remembered that she didn't even have any belongings to pack. She looked at the phone in its dock in the hallway. She could call her father and be asleep on his sofa within the hour. Maxim was behaving oddly tonight and she didn't like it. She looked at his shirt. It looked familiar. For some reason, it didn't sit right with her.

'Why is the third bedroom locked?'

'Pardon?'

'The other bedroom. The door's locked. Why?'

'Would you like to see inside?'

For the first time in her life, Paige felt uneasy in Maxim's company. 'Are you feeling all right?'

'Why wouldn't I be?'

'You just… you don't seem like yourself.'

'I'm fine. Would you like to see the room?'

Their eyes locked. Maxim didn't blink.

'All right,' she said.

Paige followed him as he led the way down the hall and up the stairs. Something was wrong. She wished her father had stayed for dinner, but couldn't explain why.

Maxim pulled a key from his pocket. He looked strange in the dark.

'You ready?'

She nodded slowly. He stepped aside and allowed her to enter. What she saw made her stop in her tracks. Cold sweat broke out all over her body.

By the flickering light of numerous candles, she saw photos of herself plastering all four walls: her as a baby, a toddler, a child, a teen, her as an adult, a mother, a widow. Her entire life was in front of her. There were photos of her at the graveyard the night she was arrested, and asleep on her sofa hugging to her chest the jumpsuit that Chloe had worn as a baby. There was a photo of her naked, taken up close – her eyes were closed in sleep.

Lit candles were dotted around the edges of the room – he had planned to show her all along. The carpet beneath her feet felt rough, and was stained with hardened, white spills.

She couldn't understand. Her thoughts refused to string together and tell her what was right in front of her.

'It's always been you,' he said, walking up behind her.

His hands slipped around her waist and pulled her gently against him.

'What?' Tears filled her eyes as she gaped at the photos. She turned around.

It was as though a completely different man stood before her – someone deranged, a terrifying stranger. The candlelight flickered in his eyes.

She looked at his shirt, and immediately knew why it was so familiar: it was Ryan's. She had bought it for him.

'Dad always tried to come between us. Locking your bedroom door, sending me away to study Christ. But our bond was too strong. It never broke, even after all these years.'

'Maxim, what is this?' She turned back to face the photographs, trying to remember the past he described. She could see her naked body in the photos. Bile crept up her throat.

'This is love,' he whispered in her ear.

She turned and backed against the wall, tears rolling down her cheeks. He stepped forward and kissed her. His warm tongue slithered slowly into her mouth. She sank her teeth into it until she tasted blood. He staggered back with bloody lips.

'You're my *brother!*'

'You love me.'

'As a *sibling!*'

'It's more than that. It's always been more.'

'No it hasn't! What the hell is wrong with you?'

'For years I've protected you, waited for you to remember.'

'You're sick. You're sick in the head!'

'Don't be like this. Not when we finally have the chance to be happy.'

'What are you talking about? This can't be happening.'

He stepped forward again, as though she wasn't looking at him in terror, as though she hadn't bitten him to be free of him. She slapped his face so hard he reeled backwards.

'You're *sick*!'

He looked at her again, his eyes filled with blind rage. 'This isn't how it was supposed to go.'

She couldn't speak. She could only stare at him, trying to understand what sort of man he was, what sickness hid beneath his skull.

'You've always been my girl. Always have. Always will. And now I have you.'

He lunged at her and pinned her against the wall. Photos of her slipped from the wall and burned against the candles. He kissed her hard, one hand around her throat, the other clawing up her T-shirt to touch her breasts. She brought her knee up into his crotch. As he staggered back, she ran for the door, only to scream out and fall back as he grabbed a fistful of her hair.

'You're finally mine again,' he spat into her ear. 'And I'm not losing you a second time. I'm going to keep you where you're safe.'

'Maxim, please!' she sobbed as he dragged her down the stairs by her hair. This was her brother, not a stranger. This madman was her own flesh and blood.

'I thought it would be enough,' he said. 'I thought it would be enough to fill the void you left in me.'

He dragged her from the stairs to the locked cupboard door beneath. She couldn't think straight; she could only cry, bent over, her hair held tight in his fist. He turned the key in the lock and pulled her up until she was standing upright, his face inches from hers. 'No one could take your place. I finally know that now.' He kissed her, and growled in frustration when she squealed, before yanking open the door to reveal a stairwell.

'You'll come around,' he said. 'You'll remember what we had, and you'll learn to love me like you used to.'

'Maxim—'

For a brief second she was in mid-air, before she crashed down onto the staircase and tumbled to the cold concrete floor. She heard a gasp and scream. Everything was spinning. Paige looked up the stairs to see Maxim slam the door shut; she heard a key turn in a lock. She could taste blood in her mouth and feel tears on her cheeks.

The room was bright – too bright. Squinting, she looked around and saw them: a woman and two children. All of them had auburn hair, pale skin, and wide eyes. The children were scared, and cowered against the woman who Paige seemed to recognise. The long red hair, the freckles on her nose and cheeks, the cool-blue of her eyes – the woman who stared back at her, the woman with a missing arm, was Chloe.

II

17

I had been back at school for less than a month, and already I longed for the next summer to come around. I trudged through the back fields, the strap on my school bag digging into my shoulder from the weight of my books. After a day of learning, writing and reading, I had to go home and do homework, as well as read three chapters of a book that I didn't even like. Walking over the bridge, I stopped halfway and looked down at the river flowing beneath my feet.

I should chuck the bloody bag in the river. I've just been studying all day, why the hell do I have to go home and do it all over again?

I imagined throwing the bag from my shoulder and into the water, and rushing to the other side of the bridge to watch the current steal away with it. I came back to reality with a sigh, and continued my trek towards home.

Walking up the lane towards the village, I wondered what Mum would cook for dinner; I felt sick with hunger. I hadn't eaten lunch – instead, I had pocketed the money Dad had given me and bought two cigarettes from Amy. I hadn't even tried smoking yet, but my friends had over the summer, and I felt left out and boring. I wondered if I could pretend I smoked without ever having to prove it in front of the group. The smell alone made me feel sick.

A car pulled up beside me and I smiled. Uncle Maxim smiled back.

'Get in, kid. I'll drop you home.'

'Thanks.'

I got into the passenger seat and dropped my bag by my feet.

'Good day?' he asked, driving on up the road.

'Kinda.'

'Sucks to be back, I bet.'

'Yeah. Summer holidays went too quickly.'

'It'll be half-term, soon.'

I nodded and looked out the window at the first signs of the village: the post office, the corner shop, the steeple of the church by my uncle's house.

'I just need to get something for your mum from home. I'll nip in and get it and then drop you back.'

'Okay.'

Anything to keep me from doing homework.

He drove on and turned down the lane towards

the vicarage. It really was quite pretty: thatched roof, brickwork painted white, surrounded by large, colourful trees that had just begun to turn with autumn.

Maxim pulled up outside the house.

'I'll be one sec. I need to find it first. If I'm not out in five minutes, come in and save me.'

I laughed and watched him enter the house before I began fiddling with the radio. I found a track I liked and relaxed into the passenger seat, looking up at the brightly coloured leaves on the trees and the clouds drifting in the sky. I closed my eyes for a second, listening to the song on the radio, humming along with the tune.

When I opened my eyes again, the sky wasn't blue, but dark grey. The radio wasn't playing anymore. Maxim hadn't come out of the house since he went inside. The front door was still ajar.

I got out, leaving my bag in the car, and headed for the door. The cold evening wind blew at my skirt and bit at my bare legs. My hair whipped against my face. When I reached the door, I pushed it wider; the hinges squealed. It was dark inside the house.

'Uncle Maxim?'

Nothing.

I stepped inside. The floorboards creaked under my feet.

'Maxim?'

I walked deeper into the house and gasped as the door

slammed shut behind me and something cracked against the side of my head.

*   *   *

The first thing I did when I opened my eyes was sit and throw up. The room was so dark it was as though I hadn't opened my eyes at all. I felt dizzy. The smell of sick was so strong that it made my eyes water. All I could hear were my own frantic breaths. Warm bile soaked through my school shirt until it stuck to my body. My head was throbbing; moving it only made me feel sick again. I tried to raise my hand to touch the wound on my head, but couldn't. Each time I tried, I heard a rattling: metal against metal; my wrists itched from a fuzzy fabric. They were individually restrained.

Maxim's house must have been broken into, but he returned home before the intruder could get away. Is Maxim in here, too?

Fuzzy handcuffs – the sex kind. One set on each wrist. I was sitting on something buoyant. I began to explore with my bare feet, until they got tangled in a thin bed sheet.

When I first opened my eyes, I had been lying down. I had enough freedom to sit up against the metal bedframe and lie back down. I moved my wrists, pulling them up and down what felt like metal poles on the bedframe.

'Hello?' My voice was shaking. I tried to clear my

throat and swallow, but my mouth was too dry. 'Maxim? Are you in here?'

A sharp pain shot inside my head, so I lay back down, wishing I hadn't thrown up on myself as it seeped through my clothes, ran down my sides and onto the bedding.

Where am I? How long have I been here?

I stared up into the darkness, trying to ignore the agony from my head. I tried to remember what had happened before I woke up there. All I could remember was walking into Maxim's house, the door slamming shut, and being hit with something. The person who attacked me had been hiding in the shadows.

I shivered in the darkness. I listened to my anxious breaths and felt tears running down my temples. I cried, longing for my mum to comfort me, to wrap her arms around me and tell me that everything was going to be okay.

I was filthy. I needed to pee so badly. My head felt as though it had been stamped on by a heavy foot. All I wanted to do was go home.

18

I woke up to darkness again. The sick had dried around my mouth and on my clothes, and stuck to the bed sheet. Pins and needles pricked at my arms. My head was still throbbing and the pain brought tears to my eyes. I promised myself not to cry again, as the old streams itched like mad, and I couldn't reach my face to scratch at them. If I didn't pee soon, I feared that my bladder would explode.

'Hello?'

Nothing.

'Is anyone in here?'

I could hear water dripping deep within the darkness.

'I… I really need to pee. I can't hold it.'

Drip. Drip. Drip.

'Please!'

I broke my promise and began to cry as hot urine wet my thighs and soaked into my skirt. It seeped into the bed and between my buttocks, down my legs and crept up my back. I cried until my pee turned cold.

Mum would be really worrying. It felt as though I had been handcuffed to the bed for days. How long had I been asleep? An hour? Five hours? A day? I wasn't sure. I wasn't sure of anything. Dozens of questions wriggled around my mind like worms in wet soil. Everything seemed sour: the taste of sick on my tongue, the scent of old pee, the body odour wafting from my armpits. The filthiness alone made me want to cry again. My head hurt, my mouth was as dry as sand, and my gut was rumbling.

My mum would have been the first person to know that I was missing – I imagined her looking at the clock on the kitchen wall and noticing that I wasn't home from school at the usual time. She would try to stay calm, and tell herself that she was overreacting, that I was probably out with friends, or had gone to a friend's house but had forgot to tell her. But then an hour would pass, and another, and then another, and Dad would get home from work, and dinner would turn cold, and I still wouldn't be home.

Go to Maxim's house, Mum. See that he's hurt, and that I've been taken somewhere. Maybe Maxim saw who hurt me. Maybe he can tell the police what the person looks like.

I tugged at the handcuffs. I tried to squeeze my hands through the cuffs, but they wouldn't fit through. The fuzz on the cuffs was so itchy. Everything was itchy. If only I could wash away the sick, the pee, the dried-up tears, my smelly armpits. I tugged harder. Nothing.

'Hello?'

Silence.

Someone must want me for something. Someone will come soon – I wouldn't have been left here to die. Would I?

'Hello?'

Scream. Scream for help.

I wanted to, but I was so frightened. The person who had cuffed me to the bed and left me in the dark wouldn't want me screaming.

'*HELP! HELP ME! PLEASE! SOMEBODY!*'

I screamed as loud as I could, a high-pitched screech that hurt my ears.

And then I heard something.

A key turned in a lock.

Door hinges creaked and light shone down a staircase.

Finally, I could see something of my surroundings: the bed was in a small, dark room, a doorway sat at the end of the bed, looking out onto a bigger room where the staircase was.

Footsteps creaked on old wooden steps. A shadowy figure came into view; whoever it was, the person was looking straight at me, handcuffed to the bed.

A light switch clicked and strip lighting in the big room began to flicker. I saw flashes of a man at the bottom of the staircase, and of the room itself, as well as the vomit that covered me. I saw a room with no windows, only walls; kitchen units lined one wall, and I noticed there was an old dark-coloured sofa in the room. The light stopped flickering, and I saw my uncle standing at the foot of the stairs, staring in at me.

'Maxim! Help me!'

I pulled at the handcuffs.

'I don't know what happened. I came in to look for you and then someone hit me over the head and I woke up here.'

Maxim stared at me calmly. He didn't rush to free me.

'You're filthy,' he said. He walked over to the kitchen sink and began to fill a washing-up bowl with water. As he squirted washing-up liquid into the bowl and took a cloth from the cupboard under the sink, I stared at him in disbelief.

Why isn't he hurrying? Why does he care that I'm so dirty? I can clean up once I'm safe!

'Maxim, we haven't got time! Help me get out of these cuffs!'

I stared at him as he turned off the tap and carried over the washing-up bowl. He rested the bowl on the bed and sat beside it, making me bounce under his weight, and began to soak the cloth in the bubbly water.

'Maxim!'

'Shh… Let me clean you up.'

He moved up the bed until he was beside me. He squeezed the cloth and brought it to my face, wiping away the tears, the crust in the corners of my eyes, and the dry sick on my chin; he rinsed the cloth in the water before using it to wipe the vomit from my hair.

I searched his face and head for injuries like mine, but couldn't find any. He was wearing different clothes and his face was freshly shaved. Nothing made sense.

He looked at my stained clothes and began to unbutton my shirt. He cleaned my chest where the sick had seeped through the fabric and hardened on my skin.

'Maxim, stop!'

'I'm sorry I was gone so long, I had to do something, but I'm here now.'

'What... what's happening?'

He rubbed the wet cloth over my body, his eyes on my skin.

'Stop it!'

'Chloe, you're filthy. I can't leave you like this.'

'Leave me? You need to get me out of here!'

'I hadn't thought about the toilet situation. I'm sorry about that. I thought you would be out for a while longer.'

I stared at him, trying to digest it all.

'I don't understand.'

'I'll have to change the bedding, too. I should have thought of that. I should've planned it better. I'm sorry.'

'What… what are you talking about? Why aren't you helping me?'

He looked into my eyes. I saw a terrifying calmness. He wasn't there to save me. He was the one who had hurt me and handcuffed me to the bed in the basement.

'You…'

'Shh. Don't get worked up again. I need to look at your head. I'll clean that up, too. I have a first aid kit. I'll go get it.'

All I could do was stare at him in horror.

Why would he do this to his own niece? This can't be real.

He shuffled down the end of the bed and stood in the main room, turning to look back at me on the bed.

'You look so much like her, you know, when she was your age.'

He turned again and went up the stairs, leaving me handcuffed to the bed, too confused to utter a single word.

* * *

Maxim didn't even undo the cuffs when he changed the bed sheets. He pulled the sheets from beneath me and had me lift myself up so he could fit the clean one to the mattress. To lift myself away from the bed, I had to press my body against his.

He cleaned my teeth and brushed my hair. He gave me a flannel to clean myself with, but he didn't turn away.

He said the wound on my head would be fine now that it had been cleaned. I wouldn't need stitches. I drank water through a straw and he fed me soup and a slice of bread. He smiled the whole time, and all I could do was stare at him, unable to believe that the man before me was my own flesh and blood, my mother's brother, the man in so many of my cherished memories. Once I was clean and fed, he dressed me in a man's checked shirt and boxers and kissed my forehead before cuffing my wrists again. He shuffled down to the end of the bed again, taking my dirty uniform with him. He stood up and leaned against the doorway.

'I'm sorry I have to keep you in those,' he said, looking at the handcuffs. 'It's only until I can trust you. I got the fuzzy kind, so they won't hurt as much.'

'I don't understand…'

I looked at my uncle through the tears that were filling my eyes. I couldn't process any of it.

'It's okay. Everything is going to be okay.'

I was so confused. The sound of his familiar voice was comforting, even though this new Maxim was terrifying me. Tears spilled down my face.

'I want my mum,' I said, and burst into tears.

'I want her, too,' he replied. 'But now I have you.'

He turned and headed up the stairs, ignoring my sobs, and turned out the light.

'No! Come back! Don't leave me in the dark!'

137

I listened to the key turn in the lock, and cried myself to sleep.

*   *   *

I could remember so many things about my uncle: the awful festive jumper he wore on Christmas Day each year, the piñata he bought for my fifth birthday party. Maxim had been there for every Christmas, every birthday, every important moment in my short life, and now he was holding me prisoner. There had never been a time when I thought he could harm me: he never disciplined me, never touched me inappropriately, never did anything to reveal the person that he was to me in the basement.

When he came down to me again, after what seemed like a lifetime since his last visit, he had a silver bowl with him and a roll of toilet paper. He promised me that he would sort something out soon, a real toilet, and ways for me to be more comfortable. He promised not to leave it so long next time. He turned his back as I used the bowl as a toilet, allowing me one free hand to wipe myself, before handcuffing me to the bedrail again. For the second time, he cleaned my teeth, brushed my hair, fed me and gave me water through a straw. I didn't ask him any questions, I was too confused, too terrified. I let him care for me, talk to me as though I wasn't his niece, and didn't cry as he walked up the stairs, turned off the light and locked the door behind him.

*   *   *

I woke up to a sharp pain in the crook of my elbow. Half asleep and confused, I saw Maxim's silhouette towering over me in the doorway, holding something sharp in his hand. I tried to ask him what was happening, what he had pricked me with, but my voice was slurred. It was as though I had slowly begun to melt. Everything turned soft until I couldn't move anymore. My entire body became heavy as I slowly returned to sleep.

*   *   *

The first thing I smelt was blood – thick, metallic blood seeping into my nostrils. I opened my mouth to speak and tasted blood on my tongue. My eyes began to flicker open and watered from the bright strip lighting above me. I was in agony, but too confused to gauge what had happened to me. My body was lying on something hard; I suddenly missed the softness of the bed. Maxim was towering over me, appearing blurry. I felt his sweat drip onto my face.

'It's nearly over. I'll give you some more drugs. You'll feel better. It's almost over now. I stopped the bleeding.'

What bleeding? What happened to me?

I felt the sting of the needle, only feeling the hot,

burning agony for a few more seconds before my eyes flickered again, and I returned to the deep, dark sleep.

*   *   *

I woke up crying from the pain; the tears were already on my cheeks. Whatever Maxim had drugged me with made me groggy, as though I had been poisoned, and every part of me felt heavy and sore. My mouth and throat were so dry that I could barely swallow, and my skin smarted all over. But none of that compared to the agony pulsing from my left elbow. I tried to move it. My left wrist wasn't handcuffed – only my right wrist, which meant I couldn't touch where it hurt to find out what had happened to my left arm. It was dark, but I had become used to that. I tried to move the fingers on my left hand, but couldn't. Everything from the elbow down was completely numb.

Am I paralysed? What has he done to me?

Warm tears streamed down my cheeks and agonised whimpers crawled up my throat. I had never felt pain like it. Even the throbbing itself hurt, as though my pulse was beating the wound; the more I panicked, the faster my pulse became, hurting me more and more. I groaned, but the noise I made seemed warped, perhaps because of the drug he had given me; I sounded terrifying, as though the moans weren't from me, but from some sort of beast.

The sound of a key entering a lock echoed from the top of the staircase, and light shone down the steps. He must have heard me. The lights flickered on as he walked down the stairs. I immediately looked down to my arm to see what he had done to me, but all I saw was a stump where the crease of my elbow should have been: no hand, no wrist, no forearm. The scream was so loud that it rang in my ears and I could taste blood at the back of my throat.

Maxim rushed to me with another syringe, whispering something, trying to comfort me, but all I could do was scream. He snatched my leg and plunged the needle into the soft side of my thigh, and struggled as I thrashed against him, screaming.

As the light began to fade, I heard him whisper: 'I had to do it. Now they think you're dead. Now you're all mine.'

19

I walked around the room in the basement for what seemed like the millionth time. It was the same circuit, round and round, all while Maxim watched me from where he sat on the bottom step of the staircase.

Day and night no longer existed for me: I stayed alone in the dark until he visited, turned on the lights that were too bright, and removed the handcuff from my right wrist so I could stretch my legs for an hour. I spoke only when spoken to. I only looked at him when I had to; I didn't ask questions anymore, because he never gave me the answers. I followed his orders, his rules, and hoped that one day I would wake up from the horrendous nightmare.

'You're getting bigger,' he said from the bottom step, eyeing my stomach as he bit into an apple.

I didn't respond, and continued to walk round and round the room at a slow pace. I listened to him chew the mouthful of apple.

'Have you felt anything? Any pain? Any movement?'

I shook my head as I walked. It was a lie. I felt the baby move all the time. This was how I defied him: I kept things from him. I refused to give him everything. He had taken my arm, my innocence, my world, but he couldn't take everything. He couldn't hear my thoughts.

For the first few years it seemed to be about control and possession, but as I began to blossom into a woman it suddenly became more, and he would visit me with different desires.

'You only have about two months left,' he said, before biting into the apple again.

I stopped in my tracks and stared at him. He looked back at me, confused.

For the first time since he took me, he had revealed information about how long I had been in the basement. For so long, I hadn't known the day of the week, the time of day. I had simply guessed. He came to me at odd intervals, so I had never been able to work out a time schedule. He must have done it on purpose, to throw me off, to keep me from knowing. I had been inside the basement at least two years before the sex started, and at least four months before he began to suspect I was pregnant, and now he knew that I had been pregnant for seven months. That meant I had been inside the basement for almost three years.

'What?' he asked. 'Is it the baby? Is it kicking?'

'I…' I lowered myself down onto the sofa, light-headed and weak. 'I've been down here for three years?'

Three birthdays had been and gone: I was seventeen years old now. Mum would be thirty-three years old, Dad would be thirty-five. Everyone in my year at school would be at college or work. The year was 2006.

'You look tired,' he said, putting the apple core on the step before standing up. 'You should go back to bed.'

He helped me up and ushered me back to bed, frowning at me when he realised that I was smiling. He cuffed my wrist to the bed and stood in the doorway, looking at me.

'I love you so much, Paige. You know that, don't you?'

'I'm not Paige,' I said through a smile. 'I'm Chloe. I'm seventeen, and I've been down here for three years.'

Maxim grabbed my ankle so fast that it made my heart jolt. His grip was tight and his eyes filled with rage.

'Say that name again and I'll break both of your ankles so that you never walk again. Is that what you want?'

I shook my head.

'What's your name?'

'Paige.'

'Who do you belong to?'

'You. I'm yours.'

He let go of my ankle, walked up the stairs and turned off the light. As I listened to him lock the door to my prison, I lay on the bed and smiled in the dark.

I am Chloe. I have been inside this basement for three years. I am seven months pregnant. He has taken my arm, my freedom, and my innocence, but he can never know my thoughts, and he will never take my baby.

*   *   *

I woke up from the sharp pain inside my belly. It was swollen and taut, and the shooting sensation burned inside me for over a minute. I sat up and went to touch my stomach, but couldn't: my right hand was cuffed, and my left hand had been taken from me a long time ago. Liquid gushed out of me and soaked the bed, as though my stomach had burst.

My waters have broken. But I thought he said I was only seven months pregnant? Why is this happening now?

Part of me was longing for the baby to arrive so I was no longer alone, hour after hour, day after day. The other part of me wished that it didn't exist – not because I didn't love the baby, but because I was too young to be a mother. What sort of life could I give the baby, living down there in the dark?

The water felt slimy and was already turning cold on my skin, but being free of it felt so good: the pressure I had been carrying all these months had finally been released. But then a new pressure began to build, as though my ribs were being pushed out of their cage and my organs were being crushed. Beads of sweat formed on my forehead as I whimpered in the dark, breathing short, fast breaths. The sharp pain shot through my stomach again, as though the baby was ripping me apart from the inside; I could feel it moving, I could feel my whole body changing, morphing for what was to come. I clenched my teeth through the pain, groaning like an injured animal, and dug the heels of my feet into the bed until the pain lessened again.

Where is he? Can't he hear me? I can't give birth on my own, with my only hand cuffed to the bed. He has to come down. He has to hear me.

I screamed out his name just before the next contraction came.

I'm going to die. The baby is going to die. Is that what is happening? Is that why it hurts so much?

Blood appeared on my bottom lip where I had sunk my teeth into it during the contraction. I screamed for Maxim again until my voice was hoarse.

For the first time since the abduction, I was happy to hear the key turn in the lock and his footsteps on the stairs.

'It's coming!'

'But it's too early – you're only seven months!'

'Maxim, please help me! It hurts!'

I was so happy to see him; so happy that I didn't have to go through it alone. His eyelids were puffy and his hair was wild, and he was dressed in grey flannel pyjamas. He rushed around the basement, disorientated from sleep, and ran the tap to fill the washing-up bowl with water. He went to find the bag he had packed for when the baby came. For months he had read books on how to care for a baby; he had learnt the stages and symptoms of pregnancy, and had watched videos on the internet to prepare for the delivery. He brought the bag over to the bed, and checked how many centimetres I was dilated; it felt like he was prodding an open wound. He rushed back to the sink to get the bowl, which he placed at the foot of the bed; he took a cloth from the bowl and sat beside me against the bedframe and pressed the cool wet cloth to my clammy forehead. He wiped it over my neck, my chest, and swollen, taut stomach. He rubbed it softly between my legs and removed the cuff from my wrist.

'It hurts so much.'

'It will be over soon. Only one more centimetre and you'll be able to start pushing.'

'Already?' I looked up at him, terrified, wishing I didn't have to push, feel the pain, and have such a responsibility.

He held my hand.

'You can do this. You're ready.'

I didn't believe him, but I didn't have a chance to reply as the next wave of agony burned in my belly as though I had been stabbed and the blade was being twisted. I gritted my teeth and groaned, digging my heels into the bed again, and squeezed Maxim's hand as hard as I could.

'You're ready to push,' he said, his breath sour from sleep.

'I can't!'

'You have to. You can do it. I have to go to the end of the bed now.'

He moved to the end of the bed and tucked towels beneath my bum and thighs. I heard the snap of disposable gloves.

'You need to push now.'

I pushed, and screamed from the pain and the pressure.

'Keep pushing. Come on.'

Sweat and tears poured down my face and my hand gripped the bed sheet until it twisted around my fist. I had to stop, to breathe, but pushed again when I felt the pressure moving downward, through me. From behind my closed eyelids, explosions of white lights flashed with the pain. I could smell blood, faeces, and sweat.

'One more push!'

I screamed, clenched my teeth until I thought they would shatter, pushed until I felt as though my head was going to explode and my belly was about to burst.

And then I heard the first cry of my baby.

20

Once I became a mother, Maxim freed me of the handcuff. I was a prisoner, but given freedom of the whole room. Being able to walk when I pleased, use a real toilet rather than the metal bowl, and wash myself rather than be washed by Maxim's hands felt so good. He had fitted a small bath and a toilet in the basement. They were old and stained, and I was only allowed cold water, but I didn't care. I would shiver in the freezing cold water and tell myself it was worth it. For the first time since he took me, I finally had some control.

I wanted to wean John from breastfeeding once Mary arrived, but Maxim was adamant that it was the best thing for John: he was getting the nourishment he needed, and he would be smarter and healthier because of it. Every time I mentioned it, Maxim read aloud articles that he had cut out of newspapers, and told me how good breast milk was for infants. I was breastfeeding two children: one newborn, and one toddler with teeth.

I sat on the rocking chair, with John suckling from one breast and Mary from the other. John would get possessive – he had never had to share his mother's milk before – but he was getting better, although I had to scold him sometimes for biting my nipple.

For three years I had swollen breasts that lactated without warning and stained the few T-shirts I had; they felt rock hard as though stones were blocking the milk ducts. A couple of times I noticed blood in the milk around the seal of John's mouth. I loved my children, but I hated feeding them. Every time I sat on the rocking chair with John on my lap and Mary held by my good arm, I had to try and calm my racing heart and brace myself for the pain.

One day, while breastfeeding my two children on the rocking chair, I worked out that I was twenty. Twenty years old with two children, both fathered by my uncle. He chose their names; he even chose mine – I wasn't Chloe anymore, I didn't dare say the word aloud. I was Paige, my uncle's property, a clone of my mum, who he had been obsessed with all his life.

I couldn't understand him. How could a man be in love with his sister? How could he imprison me – his niece – and pretend I was a younger version of my mum? How could he have babies with me? The more I tried to work it out, the less sane I felt. Trying to understand the darkness of his mind took me to places in my own that frightened me. I learnt not to question his motives, or try to understand how his brain worked. I nodded, followed orders, let him call me by my mother's name. I would do anything to survive.

I decided to stop thinking of Mum and Dad after a few years. Thinking of them just hurt too much, and watching their faces disappear from my memory was like a dagger to my heart. I could no longer remember the sounds of their voices, or what they looked like. They were disintegrating from my mind like crumbling sand, and I couldn't do anything to stop it. All I could do was force myself to think of other things.

So many memories were gone. I couldn't remember the sound of birds singing, or waves crashing on the shore; names of films and songs were muddled up. Everything was changing and there was nothing I could do as my past, and the world outside the basement walls, disappeared. All I knew then was the life I lived within the basement, day after day, night after night, with my two precious children and their father, my uncle, my worst nightmare. Everyone must have believed I was dead by then, for no one had come looking for me. Maxim was so comfortable with our life in the basement, it was as though he had nothing to fear – and that was the most terrifying thing of all.

21

The basement was always so damp in the mornings. I could see my own breath in the air. The strip lighting on the ceiling flickered. I always hated the harshness of the lighting in there; the brightness gave me headaches. My youngest son Jacob was still asleep, wrapped up in the sheet we shared when he was too ill to sleep in his cot. His pale two-year-old body looked so delicate. I slipped out from under the sheet and walked across the cold floor to the kitchen and took my shawl from the peg on the wall to wrap tightly around myself. Mary and John were still sleeping, snoozing back to back, both sucking their thumbs on the small single bed in the main living area, tucked away in the corner. John was seven and Mary had just turned five. I often dreamt of a bigger place for them to live in: their own bedrooms; carpeted floor; and window after window, rather than endless plain walls.

The children didn't know about the world outside the basement. They thought the only people who existed were themselves, their father and me. They had never seen an animal, or clouds in the sky, or breathed fresh air into their lungs; they had never seen the sun rise or set. All they knew were the walls of the room and everything in it. They were none the wiser, and seemed to exist with the innocence that I had lost when I woke up in the basement for the first time.

I boiled the kettle. Mary and John would be up soon. The sound always roused them. I used to put off having my first cup of tea of the day, just to get an hour to myself, but I craved the heat of the mug in my hand and the tea warming my throat. They would be up and wanting breakfast before I had even taken a sip. Jacob wouldn't wake for a while; he seemed to sleep more and more in those days.

Mary's eyes flickered open and focused on me. I smiled at her, and she smiled back. As I poured boiled water into the mug, I felt Mary's arms wrap around my hips. When I looked down, I saw Mary staring up at me with so much love in those dark green eyes.

What did I ever do to deserve you?

The shadows around her eyes were getting darker, or maybe her skin was getting paler. I took my mug and my clinging daughter over to the heater. Mary turned it on as we settled down in front of it and relished the orange glow bathing our cold skin. I put the mug on the floor, grabbed the blanket from the sofa, and threw it around us. We shrank inwards towards the warmth.

'When will Daddy come home?'

'Dinnertime. Like every day.'

'Sometimes he is here in the morning.'

'Only if he is so tired he falls asleep. We don't need him to be here every night anyway, do we? He snores.'

Mary giggled as I mimicked the sound he made.

'Where does Daddy go when he's not here?'

'To work.'

'What's that?'

'It's how he earns money to pay for our food and our clothes.'

She thought about it, while staring into the orange glare of the heater.

'Where does Daddy sleep?'

'Daddy has his own room. Like this one.'

'Where?'

'Above us.'

She frowned and looked up at the cracked ceiling and the wooden rafters. Telling Mary that her father lived above us was like telling a young girl from the outside world that her father had a house on Mars.

'Can we go up there?'

'It's only for Daddy.' I couldn't talk about it anymore;

my throat was tightening at the thought of the outside world.

'Can I have some?' Her orange eyes flickered towards the mug.

'It's hot. Give it a minute.'

She nodded and leaned her head against my chest. Her shoulder pressed against the bruise on my ribs, which made me flinch.

'Why was Daddy angry?'

'It doesn't matter now. Here, have some tea, but blow on it first.'

Mary sat up and blew on the surface of the tea before she took a sip, with the mug cupped in her small, pale hands. She looked up at me with a satisfied, milky smile.

You're my everything.

Jacob began to cough; the phlegm crackled in his small lungs.

'When will Jacob get better?'

'Soon.'

'He isn't fun anymore.'

'He's tired, sweetheart. Being sick makes people tired.'

'But he has been sick for ages. I think he's faking.'

'Don't be silly. He will be better soon and will be lots of fun again.'

'I'm hungry,' John said from behind us, sleepily rubbing his eyes awake.

'Good morning to you, too.'

I stood up and put my mug of tea on the table so I could ruffle his hair.

'Cereal?'

'Yes, please,' they both said. They knew to be polite.

I leaned down to get the box of cereal from the cupboard and winced at the pain from my bruised ribs, sucking air through gritted teeth. Jacob coughed in his sleep, and each breath he took seemed to sound wheezier than the last.

I knew it would be over soon. I knew our lives were about to get worse.

22

The recycled air was heavy and stale, meaning I could never quite catch my breath. I didn't do much with my days: I tended to the children, I cleaned the basement and forever swept up mice droppings that were always replaced if I dared to turn away. I cooked; I waited for Maxim to return. Even though I was mostly idle, I was always exhausted – we all were. It was as though the unnatural light leeched the life from our skin and bones, or the trapped air was toxic, killing us with each breath we took.

'Mum...'

Mary's voice broke me out of one of my idle trances. I had been sitting in the rocking chair, staring at the wall, imagining a window that looked out over rolling fields and a cloudless blue sky. I envied the children sometimes. They had no idea what they were missing.

'Yes, darling?'

'Jacob is bleeding.'

She looked even paler than usual. Worry plagued her eyes.

My stomach clenched like a fist. By the look in Mary's eyes, it was bad.

I rushed to the bedroom and saw Jacob lying on the white sheets; blood ran from his nose and onto the sheets. He was covered in beads of sweat. He hadn't looked too bad when I settled him down for his nap.

'Jacob!'

I climbed onto the bed and took him in my arms. Blood stained my T-shirt. Mary waited at the end of the bed with tears in her eyes.

'Get me a damp cloth, Mary.'

She nodded quickly and rushed out of sight.

I looked down at Jacob: eyes closed, mouth open, bloody rivers running down to his chin.

'I'm here, baby, I'm here.'

The heat practically radiated from him, and his skin felt clammy. I took off his pyjamas to keep him cool and held him to my chest; the pyjamas were damp with sweat and blood. His skin was hot, but his sweat was cold. His heart was racing so fast, and I could see his eyes were moving behind their lids.

Mary ran back with the wet cloth. It was soaked and dripped on the floor.

'Thank you, sweetheart,' I said, as I tried to smile. I

wrung the cloth and held it to his forehead. 'Go and play, Mary. There isn't anything to worry about.'

'I'm sorry,' Mary said, her bottom lip quivering.

'What for?'

'I said he was faking. I didn't mean it.'

'Sweetheart, that doesn't matter. You're a brilliant sister. Now go and play with John. Jacob's fine now. I'll look after him.'

Mary wiped her eyes as the tears fell; I could tell she longed for a cuddle, but she knew that Jacob needed me more. She turned away sniffling.

I wiped the blood away from Jacob's face with the damp cloth, and then the back of his neck, his arms, his chest, in the hope that it would cool him down.

'I love you so much,' I whispered.

Slowly, his eyes began to open. He looked up at me from my lap. He was so tired, and so weak, that I couldn't help but tear up at the sight of him. It was as though he was asking me: *Why? Why is this happening?*

All I wanted to do was make him better, to rid his lungs of the infection that seemed to be drawing the life from him. I vowed to find a way to save us all. I didn't know how; I didn't know when – but I knew that I had to try, and soon.

23

I hid beneath the basement stairs and told the children we were playing a game. Once Daddy came down, John and Mary had to tell him I was sleeping, and they had drawings to show him. They drew the pictures especially, working on them all day as I crouched beneath the stairs with Jacob held to me with my good arm, waiting to hear the key turn in the lock. I waited there for hours, longing to pee, to eat, but I feared that the moment I did so, he would appear at the top of the stairs and I would miss my chance.

I had been torn: if I wanted to save Jacob, I had to leave John and Mary behind. There was no way all of us could escape. If I waited any longer, Jacob might not make it. I stayed up all night trying to figure out a way for all of us to leave the basement, but it couldn't be done: I had to leave them behind.

I heard the key turn in the lock and my mouth instantly

became dry. I listened to his feet on the stairs, coming closer and closer until he was right above my head, and then I saw his feet on the stairs before me, and heard him talking with the children as he reached the ground. They did what I told them to do – they said I was sleeping and took him to their drawings, his back to the stairs. My heart was racing and sweat covered my body. I was so frightened, I wanted to stay with the children, but then I felt Jacob struggling to breathe, and I knew I had to try. I had to save him.

I emerged from beneath the stairs with my eyes on his back, terrified that he would turn around and spot me, or see me moving from the corner of his eye. I placed one bare foot on the first step. I stepped again, and again, climbing higher and higher up the stairs, closer to the door, the nearest I had been to freedom in ten years. My heart was pounding hard and echoing in my ears. We were going to make it. And then Jacob began to cough. I turned to see Maxim's eyes on me. I ran up the stairs, waiting to hear his heavy feet bounding up the steps behind me, waiting for his hand to snatch my shirt and pull me back down. I positioned Jacob so I could reach for the door handle, and grabbed it.

As tears began to fill my eyes, I heard Maxim laughing at the bottom of the stairs. I turned, defeated, and saw his wide grin; he was laughing so hard that tears came to his eyes.

'You didn't really think I'd leave the door unlocked, did you?'

*   *   *

I knew exactly what he had planned for me, even before he opened the cupboard below the sink and turned back around with the bottle of bleach and the toothbrush covered in old blood and yellow crust.

He slammed the bottle on the table in front of me.

'You know what I have to do.'

He had to punish me for trying to escape. He had already told me what he would do to the children if I tried to escape again. But still, it wasn't enough. I had to be taught a lesson.

He opened the bottle of bleach and squeezed the yellow cream onto the toothbrush.

'Open.'

I closed my eyes and opened my mouth.

The worst part was waiting for the bleach to hurt. At first, it only tasted rancid, but then it began to burn my gums and tongue, and then the agony would come.

I felt the toothbrush pass my lips, and the bleach began to burn. He brushed so hard I could taste blood with the first few thrusts. I winced and whimpered, so he did it harder, until the toothbrush was hitting the back of my throat and making me gag. The nerves in my teeth began to react to the bleach with painful shocks, as though I had bitten into an electrical cord. Tears streamed down my face and I heard the children crying. He liked it when they watched – it taught them to stay in line and know who was the boss. I choked when he squirted bleach from the bottle straight into my mouth. I couldn't take it anymore. I opened my eyes and looked into his, at the smile on his face, and tried to pull away. His hand snatched my jaw.

If I swallow the bleach I might die, I thought to myself, longing for the escape. *But I can't leave the children. They need me.*

I let him throw me to the ground and straddle me. He pulled the toothbrush free from my mouth and covered my lips, trapping the bleach inside. I screamed behind his hand, which made the bleach bubble and swish around my mouth, sear my gums, pierce the nerves.

I thought he would never stop. I thought this was the time he would finally kill me. But then he took his hand away.

Bleach and blood shot out of my mouth like vomit. I coughed and heaved. A puddle of bleach and blood grew on the floor beneath me, but my mouth still burned, the shocks were still agonising, and the tears continued to flow. Yellow and red saliva slid out of my mouth like a slug's slime and joined the puddle beneath me.

'You know what I have to do if you try this again.'

I did know. I couldn't risk the lives of my children. I would never try to escape again.

24

Jacob's health had worsened. He hadn't eaten for two days, and had only managed a few sips of water. He was so thin and so weak that he hardly opened his eyes anymore, as though even the thought of it was exhausting.

I hadn't got out of bed. I did nothing but hold Jacob, stroke his hair, and cry silently so Mary and John wouldn't hear me.

It hurt to speak. There were so many ulcers in my mouth from the bleach that my cheeks swelled up. My throat was burnt and my gums wouldn't stop bleeding.

Please don't die. Please don't leave me. Please don't break my heart.

Each breath he took wheezed in and out through his mouth, as though his airways were slowly closing shut.

Hurry up and come home, I thought, as though Maxim

would hear my thoughts and come home with the antibiotics he promised to get. *Don't let it be too late.*

It was the basement. I hated it. It was damp, deprived of natural light and hidden away from fresh air and the big wide world.

Jacob was dying, and I had no way of stopping it.

He was so limp and he hardly moved. Each breath seemed to be more difficult than the last. Tears streamed down my cheeks, and one landed on Jacob's face. I wiped it away and stroked his hair while I took in the sight of his angelic features; I knew that one day I would only see his face in my dreams. I ran my fingertips over his face, feeling his thin eyebrows, the curves of his eye sockets, his button nose, the arches of his lips, and the softness of his cheeks.

'Please don't feel any more pain, Jacob. You don't deserve it.'

I sobbed silently, my chest aching as though my heart had truly broken, and held him tight to my chest. My tears ran down his face as I held him to me.

The door opened, but Mary and John didn't rush to the bottom of the stairs to greet their father like they usually did. They knew something was wrong. I listened to his footsteps and the creaking of the staircase. He didn't say a word. Maxim appeared in the doorway of the bedroom and looked in at us: a mother clutching her dying son, rocking and sobbing silently. He was a dark silhouette without a face. I couldn't see his expression and I didn't care. I hated him for not bringing the medicine sooner. He had said he could steal some when he visited Christian patients at the hospital. He had taken too long. This was on him.

He held a box of medicine in one hand and a bouquet of tulips in the other. Flowers to apologise for the bleach in my mouth, as though flowers and a smile would make the act, the memory, the pain, disappear.

'I'll deal with it,' he said, coldly.

'No! Not yet. He isn't going yet.'

'Paige—'

'I said *no!* You are not taking him from me yet.'

I held him tight and rested my head against Jacob's. Maxim left the doorway and began talking to the children quietly.

I won't let him take Jacob away.

I couldn't quieten my sobs any longer and wailed in agony, lying down on the mattress with Jacob in my arms, my tears dampening his hair.

It wasn't long before Maxim appeared in the doorway again. He was coming for Jacob.

'Not yet.'

He wasn't listening. He was going to take him away.

'I said not *yet!* He's not dead yet!'

He lunged forward and I held onto Jacob as tight as I could.

'You can't take him! You can't have him yet! Listen to me! Please, listen to me!'

My head jolted back as his fist smacked my jaw. There was a cracking sound. I was instantly disorientated, the room was almost spinning, but I could feel Jacob leaving my arms.

'NO! PLEASE, DON'T TAKE HIM FROM ME!'

I screamed, I begged, I tried to get up. Another punch to my face threw me back into the wall. The room spun and I instantly felt sick. Blood filled my mouth. His shadow wasn't there anymore. I could hear the staircase creaking under heavy feet.

'BRING HIM BACK! PLEASE, DON'T TAKE HIM AWAY FROM ME!'

I lay down and sobbed, screaming into the sheets, turning them red with the blood that poured from my mouth.

25

I sobbed until I fell asleep, or perhaps the punches knocked me unconscious. I blinked quickly to unstick my eyelids from the dried tears. The memory of Jacob leaving the basement hit me within seconds, and the sorrow weighed down on me so hard that I struggled to breathe.

My jaw felt broken; the skin was swollen and hot, and my mouth still tasted of blood. My lip had split with the second punch. I licked the scab and tasted the old blood on my tongue.

I looked into the other room: Mary and John were asleep, but the lights were still on. A bouquet of tulips was lying on the dining table, drying out, dying like everyone who inhabited the basement. Innocence didn't belong there; it couldn't survive. We would all die within those walls, except for him. I had so many nightmares about him locking the door to the basement and never coming back, leaving us to starve to death, locked in our own hell with no way to escape, our bodies left to rot. Maybe he wouldn't be that cruel. Maybe he would decide to let us die as we slept from a gas leak or breathing in smoke from a fire. Either way, cruel or not, I felt it was inevitable: we would all die and he would survive unpunished and unscathed. He was the monster from under my bed, the villain in my dreams, and the man who took everything from me – and would be the one to take my life.

I took a pair of scissors from the kitchen drawer and unwrapped the flowers. One by one, I chopped at the petals and the stems; chunks of petals fell to the floor and the blades scratched the table top. I chopped wildly as tears streamed down my face, until the bouquet was a pile of sheared leaves and petals.

Him. This is all because of him.

Hatred filled every part of me until I was shaking with rage. I longed to break down the walls, snatch up my children and run. Run until we were free of him. He was poisonous, toxic – everyone around him died.

I heard the clicking of the lock on the door and instantly became scared again. I grabbed the bin and put it by the table so I could brush the chopped flowers into it. When I turned around, he had entered the basement and was sitting on the sofa. He looked utterly defeated. I couldn't stop thinking of Jacob: what had Maxim done? Where was our son?

'Why?' he said, his voice breaking. 'Why us?

You, I thought. *This is all because of you.*

I stayed at the table, watching him, waiting for his anger to emerge, but instead, he cried. His shoulders shook as he sobbed into his hands. It was the first time that I had ever seen him cry.

He came towards me, tears shimmering on his cheeks, and dropped to his knees. He wrapped his arms around my waist, held me, and sobbed into my T-shirt.

Jacob is dead.

I hated myself for it, but I stroked his hair, tended to him as he cried, and found myself whispering, 'I don't know why.'

I stood there as Maxim held me, sobbing into me, with tears of my own rolling down my cheeks.

We will never escape you.

I listened to him sob, wishing I had the strength to break his neck, to free the children and myself of his hold on us. But instead, I stroked his hair and continued to whisper reassurances to him. Even when I had nothing left to give, he still had me in the palm of his hand.

26

John and Mary kept asking me where Jacob had gone. They had heard me screaming and saw their father carry Jacob in his arms as he went up the stairs and locked the door behind him. What could I say? That the only way either of them would leave the basement was when they were dying like Jacob?

They stopped asking me when they noticed me crying. They played quietly on the floor. I sat in the rocking chair and rocked back and forth, thinking of Jacob's first words, first steps, his dark green eyes and his heart-melting smile. I would never let myself forget his face; I might have lost the memory of my mother and father, but I wouldn't lose Jacob.

Maxim hadn't been down to the basement for a few days. He must have known that he wasn't wanted, that his face made me feel ill. I began to fear that he would never come back, that he had left us to die.

For the first time in ten years, I daydreamed about murdering Maxim. I considered how I would do it, what weapon I would use. I had always thought of escaping from him, but never killing him; I wasn't sick like Maxim. Now I wanted him dead.

I told myself that Maxim couldn't keep us inside the basement forever, however hard he tried – that one day we would be free. I had to believe it. But how would I protect the children?

The key turned in the lock, but the children stayed on the floor by my feet. For the first time, they were hearing the voice of another person: a woman was screaming, followed by scuffling and voices at the top of the stairs.

'You'll come around,' Maxim said. 'You'll remember what we had, and you'll learn to love me like you used to.'

'Maxim—' the woman's voice said.

A body was hurled down the staircase and flew through the air before landing on the stairs with a hard thud. The woman tumbled down the last few steps and crashed onto the concrete floor.

I darted to the floor and held my children to me. We all stared at the mysterious woman lying on the floor as the key turned in the lock at the top of the stairs.

She had red hair like us. She was groaning, only just feeling the pain from her fall. As the woman looked around, dazed, her eyes met mine, and we stared at each other, remembering the features we had both lost from our memories. For the first time in ten years, I was looking into my mother's eyes. Our faces crumpled, and tears filled our eyes and spilled down our cheeks.

'Is… is it really you?' Mum said.

I nodded furiously, trying not to sob. 'Mummy, you found me. You finally found me!'

We rushed into each other's arms and held each other so tight that I could barely breathe. Memories flooded back to me as I sank into the familiar shape of my mum's body, just like I had ten years before – before I became a young woman, a mother. We sobbed in each other's arms as the children watched, confused and terrified; they stared at the first person they had ever seen who wasn't a sibling or a parent.

'I have my girl back!' my mum cried. 'I finally have you back!'

III

27

Paige had thought she would never see her daughter again. She had accepted that her daughter was dead, after years of doubt and denial, only to discover that her brother – her own flesh and blood – had taken her and kept her in his basement for ten whole years. Whenever she had visited her brother in his home, she'd had no idea that her daughter was so close to her, so within her reach, hidden beneath the floorboards. He had watched Paige fall to pieces, he had comforted her – yet he had been the cause of the grief and the agony, the reason her whole world had been torn apart.

For ten minutes the mother and daughter held each other tight, unable to speak in proper sentences, their words lost to weeping. Paige felt her daughter's long hair in her hands, she felt the beat of her heart against her own chest: Chloe was alive.

She pulled away and touched her daughter's cheek,

staring at every feature, every freckle on her pale skin. Her eyes, framed by long, auburn eyelashes, were still so blue, offset by the bruises and split, swollen lip. Chloe was no longer the little girl Paige had known: she was a twenty-four-year-old woman, a mother: and, from the pain in her eyes, a tortured one.

'How?' was all she could say, with the taste of tears on her lips.

'I don't know,' Chloe replied, because it was so surreal to both of them.

'All this time?'

Chloe nodded, tears trickling down her cheeks. And then her eyes came alive. 'My babies. You must meet my babies.'

She turned and looked over to the children, who were hiding beneath the dining table and peering out at their mother and the stranger.

Paige took in the sight of them: both had red hair like their mother, but were cursed with Maxim's green eyes.

'John, Mary, come out and meet my mum. Your grandmother.'

Grandmother. I'm a grandmother.

'Nanny,' Paige said. 'Grandmother makes me sound so old.'

They laughed, with eyes still shining with tears.

'Come on out,' Chloe beckoned with a comforting smile.

The young girl came out first and ran to the safety of her mother.

'This is Mary,' Chloe said. The child stared up at Paige.

The boy followed and sat beside his mother on the concrete floor.

'And this is John.' Chloe brushed his fringe away from his startling green eyes.

John. Mary. Straight from the Bible. I wouldn't expect any less from Maxim.

'This is Nanny Paige; she is my mummy, just like I'm yours.'

They looked up at their mother, and then at Paige, trying to figure it out: other people had mothers, not just them.

'Why haven't we met her before?' John asked her.

'It's a long story, but she's here now.'

'Is she Daddy's mummy, too?' Mary asked.

Chloe looked at Paige.

No, Paige thought. *He's my brother. Your mother's uncle.*

'No, just mine.'

Paige couldn't stop thinking about how they had been conceived. It took every ounce of strength to fight back the tears.

I am going to kill him.

'Mummy and Nanny have a lot of talking to do,' Chloe said. 'So you both should sit and play.'

Paige stood up and was horrified to see the children cower below her. She apologised as she backed away and sat on the old, worn sofa. The children took their toys to the furthest corner of the basement, so they could watch her from a safe distance. Chloe sat next to her mother on the sofa, and they instantly held hands. Paige stared at the stump where the rest of her daughter's arm should have been. Her hand shook as it reached out to touch it, her fingertips stroking the skin on the stump. She couldn't even begin to imagine how Maxim had severed the bone, or had even been able to conjure up the idea, let alone put it into action.

Paige had never had to digest so much information at once: her daughter wasn't dead, she had been taken by her uncle and kept in a windowless basement for ten long years. Maxim had been there to support her when Chloe went missing. He had told her everything was going to be okay, when he had known all along that Chloe was alive, right beneath the floorboards of his house. Paige had been staying in the house since hers had burned down, and she'd had no idea that her daughter was hidden directly beneath her feet.

'I can't believe you're here,' Chloe said, unable to take her eyes off her mother's face, as though if she dared to blink, she would vanish for good.

'I can't believe you're alive.'

They held each other for a few minutes, and the tears

flowed again. They wiped their cheeks dry and both took deep breaths.

'How did this happen? Why?'

'I was walking home from school and Maxim pulled up beside me and offered to drive me home. He said he had to stop at his house first, to pick up something for you, and left me in the car outside. He didn't come back out again, and when I went looking for him, he hit me over the head and I woke up down here.'

Chloe kept talking, divulging everything that happened to her once she woke up in the basement, whispering for the sake of the children.

'We both lost control of our lives that day,' she said. 'I lost my freedom, and he lost himself to his obsessions and desires. He had no more control over his life than I did mine. We were both prisoners from then on.'

Paige couldn't hold back the tears, they flowed and flowed, but she didn't make a sound. Her bottom lip trembled, and bile sat at the back of her tongue, ready to lurch up and out of her mouth, but she waited until Chloe was finished with her story before she ran to the kitchen sink and vomited. The children cowered in the corner as she ran.

'I'm so sorry,' she said, with bile stringing from her lips. She ran the tap, drank, and rinsed away the sick from the sink bowl.

'I don't know how he could do this,' she said, feeling

Chloe's hand rest on her back. She stood up and looked around the room, taking in the sight of the concrete walls and floors, spider webs and mice droppings, an old bed in a room of its own. She doubled over and vomited into the sink again. Her daughter had been handcuffed to that bed for three years.

Chloe cleaned her up and ushered her back to the sofa. Paige was shaking violently.

'Where's Dad?' she asked.

Paige shook her head. 'I'm so sorry.'

Chloe flinched and her eyes began to glisten again. 'How?'

'He couldn't take it anymore.'

Paige didn't need to say another word. Chloe nodded, and big, silent tears fell onto her lap.

'Why now? Why has he brought you down here now?'

My own brother told me he was in love with me, showed me the shrine he had created in my honour, and touched me, kissed my lips, groped my body, wanting me – his own sister.

'I don't know.'

'Will he come for you again? Take you away?'

'He can't, not now that I know you're alive down here. He knows I won't leave here without you or your children.'

And then she realised: Maxim never planned to let her go. He wanted to keep her down there with Chloe and their children forever.

28

Maxim paced the room with tears of frustration filling his eyes, as he tried to figure out how it had all gone wrong. Did she not remember the love they used to have? All those nights he crept into her room and made love to her? She had to remember. He was certain that she did. If it hadn't been for their father, they would still be together. They would have had their own children. He wouldn't have had to take Chloe. She must see that; she would, with time.

He took a swig of Scotch from the bottle and decided to head upstairs to her room – the room he had dedicated to her. He looked at all of the photos, the candles still lit and flickering. Hundreds of Paiges stared back at him from the walls: they were laughing at him, taunting him. He could hear her voice in his head.

'You're sick. You're sick in the head!'

He hit his head with his fists, and tried to beat the words from his brain.

'No! She loves me!'

He snatched at the faces on the walls, tore her eyes off him, ripped up her smile, punched a photo of her face until his fist broke through the plaster on the wall. He kicked and yelled and cried, destroying the room he had devoted to her – the one place where he felt at peace – until he was lying on the floor, sobbing like a child, holding the one photo of her that he couldn't bear to rip: the photo of the two of them, smiling into the camera, her with freckles on her nose from the summer sun, him with the first few strands of facial hair on his chin. She had loved him then. She had beckoned him into her room, into her bed, whispering inside his head, telling him what she wanted him to do to her. She loved him then, and she would love him again; he just had to give her time.

And then the doorbell rang.

29

Paige watched as Chloe tucked her children into bed and gave them each a kiss.

There was still no sign of Maxim. It had been at least three or four hours since he had locked her in the basement. She couldn't even begin to wonder what he was doing up there above them. She'd had no idea he was capable of this – how could she try and figure out what he planned to do next?

She sipped at the mug of tea Chloe had made for her, still attempting to digest it all, and tried to think of a way to escape.

'They are used to the lights,' Chloe said as she came back and sat with her mother on the sofa. 'They nap in the day, we all do; it makes the time go faster.'

'I can't even begin to imagine how you've managed to cope down here for so long. You're so strong.'

'I don't know, either,' she said before looking over to

her children tucked up in the bed. 'They don't know any different.'

'Is he… good with them?'

'He doesn't hurt them. They love him.'

'But he hurts you.'

'I'm not you. Even he knows that, however hard he tries to believe it. The truth upsets him.'

Paige stared into space as she tried to fathom her brother's obsession with her, his mindset, his ability to do what he has done for so long.

'Don't waste your time trying to work him out,' Chloe said, as if reading her mother's mind. 'I stopped a long time ago. I don't even think he understands himself.'

Paige suddenly sat up straight. 'Did you hear that?' She looked up at the ceiling.

'Hear what?'

'It sounded like a bell.'

Paige got up from the sofa and crept up the wooden steps. She could hear a man's voice on the other side of the door.

She sat on the steps so her eyes were level with the floor and looked through the crack underneath the door. Shoes passed.

'Where is she, Maxim?'

Dad.

'She's safe.'

'I want to see her.'

'You can't separate us, Dad. Not like before. She's mine – she always has been. I won't let you come between us again.'

'I thought you'd changed... I thought you had got better, overcome these delusions, this obsession—'

'Obsession? It's love.'

'She's your sister!'

'You don't understand what we have. You never have.'

'We were protecting her when we sent you away, your mother and I, but we were trying to protect you, too. We were giving you a second chance. We shouldn't have. She is in danger because we let her down; I let her down. I let you get to her.'

'I won't let you separate us again.'

'Where is she?'

'Somewhere you can't reach her.'

'DAD!' she yelled for him from behind the door, and saw his shoes turn towards the door.

'Paige?'

'In here!'

He turned the handle just before something smashed and glass showered down on the floor on the other side of the door. Paige watched in horror from underneath the door as they fought and scuffled on the other side. She could hear punches, groans, falling objects.

'Leave him alone!' she screamed from behind the door.

'No!' her father yelled.

And then she heard the gunshot.

Her ears rang so loud that she couldn't hear herself screaming. Her tears ran from her chin and onto the wooden steps.

Drops of blood began fall onto the floorboards just outside the door. Her father's face appeared at the crack under the door, hitting the floorboards with a loud thud. His eyes were open and stared at her lifelessly from the other side. Blood pooled beneath him and crept under the door.

Paige screamed and screamed as she stared into her father's vacant eyes.

'He can never come between us again, Paige,' Maxim said from behind the door. 'Now we can be happy.'

30

'We're getting out of here, Chloe. I won't let him hurt you anymore,' Paige said, pacing the room and shaking violently.

Chloe looked at her mother with what looked like pity, as though Paige didn't understand the situation she was in. 'He won't let us leave.'

'Of course he won't. We'll make him.'

'He said that…' Chloe looked over to the children, who had managed to fall asleep again after they woke up to the gunshot and Paige's screams. Chloe lowered her voice to a whisper. 'He said he would kill the children if I tried to escape.'

'Chloe, I won't let that happen.'

'But I can't take that chance.'

'I'm your mother. I will make sure you and the children get out of here alive.'

'Mum… He will never let us leave – any of us.'

She spoke so surely that Paige began to doubt herself.

She couldn't escape the memory of her father's lifeless eyes staring at her through the crack beneath the door; the bloody puddle forming around him. They had spoken of a past that Paige couldn't remember. What did Maxim do to be sent away? What did he do to her?

They had been waiting for hours for Maxim to come down after murdering his father, but he never showed.

'I had a third child until a few days ago,' Chloe said, her face painted with pain.

Had. The word stung at Paige's chest.

'Jacob, his name was. He was dying. He was getting worse and worse each day until…' she hesitated as tears filled her eyes. 'Maxim took him. The only way we will leave the basement is if we are dying or already dead.'

Paige was speechless. She imagined her brother taking the dying boy from the basement, carrying him up the stairs, and… what did he do with him?

And then she remembered the boy on the front of the newspapers in the hospital. The lockdown. The media frenzy. The boy without a family. Those piercing green eyes.

'How old was Jacob?'

'Two,' Chloe said, wiping he tears from her cheeks.

'Green eyes? Red hair?'

Chloe looked strange, as though she wouldn't dare

believe that there was hope that her son was still alive.
'Yes.'

'I think I know where he is.'

Chloe looked away, as though she wouldn't let herself believe it. When she looked back at her mother, tears were flowing again, and a smile had spread across her face.

'Jacob's alive? How? Where is he?'

'There was a boy at the hospital. He had been left outside the entrance with pneumonia. His face is featured on the front page of every newspaper in the country.'

'But what if it isn't Jacob?'

'Two years old, no known relatives, green eyes and red hair? I really think it's him, Chloe.'

Chloe broke down and fell into her mother's embrace as tears streamed into her relieved smile.

'Jacob's alive!'

As she rocked her daughter, Paige's eyes filled with tears as well.

'I have to find him. I have to get to him,' Chloe said, wiping her cheeks; she looked exhausted.

'You will Chloe, I promise.'

'When I first woke up here, he left me for a long time,' Chloe said. 'I don't think he will be coming down for a while. Do we wait? Do we rest?'

'I can't let my guard down. That's what he wants.'

'Do you mind if I rest?' Chloe asked. 'You don't have

to sleep, but you could lie with me. I have to be strong and ready to go to Jacob.'

Now that they had been reunited, neither of them could bear the thought of being apart. Paige nodded.

Chloe led her to the bed, the very same bed that she had been handcuffed to for three years. Chloe got on the bed and lay down. She beckoned her mother to join her. Paige slipped off her shoes and climbed onto the bed, unable to forget that it was the bed where her daughter's children had been conceived.

'I'll still be here when you wake up,' Paige said.

Chloe rested her head on her mother's lap and closed her eyes. A faint smile rested on her lips, as though she was thinking of Jacob alive and well. Paige stroked Chloe's hair until she fell asleep.

As Paige sat there on the bed and stared out into the basement, she began planning how she would kill her brother for what he had done. It wasn't too long before her eyes began to flicker, begging for rest, and she unwillingly allowed her guard to drop and fell asleep.

31

*T*he moment Paige walked through the door she knew something was wrong. She could sense the tension in the air, the silence that had fallen on the house the moment the key entered the lock in the front door.

Mum and Dad knew.

Maxim was behind her, standing in front of the open door. He didn't follow Paige inside at first. He sensed it too.

'Don't say a word,' he told her. 'Let me handle it.'

He shut the door and they walked down the quiet hallway and into the living room. Mum and Dad were waiting.

'Paige, can we speak to you alone please?' Dad said.

Paige hesitated, waiting for Maxim's permission, but he wouldn't be that brazen − not in front of them. She nodded and sat down on the opposite sofa. Maxim went to sit beside her.

'We'd like to speak to Paige alone, Maxim.'

'Whatever you have to say, you can say it in front of me.'

'Maxim,' Dad warned.

Maxim was nineteen, and had been taller and stronger than their father for some time; they stared at each other, the tension growing thicker. Finally, Maxim stood and left the room, but shot Paige a look of warning before he closed the door. Paige knew he would be listening on the other side.

She didn't look at her parents, but at the floor, waiting for them to say the words. She couldn't tell them the truth. Maxim said their parents would cut them out of the family. They wouldn't understand. She couldn't lose her parents, so she had to lie.

She heard her dad sigh heavily, sadness hanging heavy in the sound.

'We know you're pregnant, Paige.'

Tears began to sting at her eyes. She tried to blink them away. Her face felt hot and red, and her palms began to sweat.

'Honey, talk to us,' her mum said.

Paige could only shake her head, and when she did, tears slid down her cheeks.

He was listening on the other side of the door. She couldn't talk, not with him so close.

'Is the father a boy from school?'

She shook her head.

'Who is it, Paige? Who's the father?'

Her throat was burning from holding back the sob that longed to claw out of her. The truth was there, stuck in her throat, longing to climb up and out into the open, to be heard. Her whole body was shaking.

They wouldn't give up. Not until they knew. She had to tell them.

She whispered his name.

'Who? Speak up, honey. We're not angry. We just need to know.'

Her bottom lip began to quiver. She couldn't see through the tears.

She whispered again, terrified to say it, for Maxim to hear her. What would he do to her if he heard? Would Mum and Dad really throw them out and never talk to them again?

'Paige, talk to us.'

She couldn't breathe. Her throat was tight. Her chest was on fire. Tears flowed and flowed as she parted her lips to form his name.

'Maxim.'

Paige jolted awake. All of the resurfacing memories had bled into her dreams, and she had been crying in her sleep. She remembered everything.

How could I have forgotten? How is that possible?

And then she recalled where she was: the basement. Chloe wasn't beside her.

'Chloe?'

The basement was as dark as night. She tried to leave the bed, but couldn't. She was strapped to the bed by her wrists: one wrist in handcuffs, and the other, in the plaster cast, stuck to the bedframe by duct tape.

'Maxim?' her voice was timid, terrified. Tears streamed down her cheeks. Sweat covered her body. She was withdrawing from the pills. Her head was pounding and her heart was racing.

'Maxim, answer me.'

'It didn't have to be like this.'

The sound of his voice from within the darkness made her flinch. He was in the room somewhere, taunting her.

'Where's Chloe? Where are the children?'

'They're here.'

She couldn't hear them. Either he was lying or they were gagged, or worse.

'You can't keep us shut in here forever.'

'I'll find a way. We can make it work.'

'We aren't possessions, Maxim, we're *people*. You can't keep us locked down here for your own pleasure.'

'You are all I've ever wanted. If only you had cooperated, none of this would have happened. Chloe would have never been born. You would never have met Ryan. It could have been you and me, and *our* children.'

'Maxim, I'm your *sister*. We share parents, DNA – it's not right.'

'We had a child before.'

Paige knew Chloe would be confused on hearing this.

She had no idea about the life Paige had had to endure before she met Ryan, before Chloe was born.

'It's dead. I had an abortion. I got that thing out of me as quickly as I could.'

'You don't mean that. Mum and Dad made you.'

'They didn't make me do anything. I was glad to be free of it, of that *thing* that you put there, growing inside of me. It repulsed me because it was a part of you. I remember everything, I remember it all.'

She could see the memories playing in her mind: how he had controlled her every move, never letting her be alone, and how he had told her what she could wear, what she could eat, who she could see – controlling her entire life right before their parents' eyes, but they couldn't see it.

'The children can hear you. Is that really what you think of them?'

'They are nothing like you. They are as kind and beautiful as their mother. You're nothing to do with who they are.'

Her mind wouldn't stop remembering. She saw her old bedroom, dark with the night, as she waited for Maxim to creep into her bedroom and shut the door behind him. She would wipe the tears away before he came too close. Her parents had had no idea what happened to her when they fell asleep.

'Mum and Dad thought I was shy,' she was laughing, a

deranged sound in the darkness, and tears streamed down her cheeks. 'I wasn't *shy*, I was terrified. I couldn't do anything without your permission. I didn't have friends, I didn't have thoughts of my own, I didn't have anything. When I walked to and from school, you were there to drop me off and pick me up. When I went shopping, you were right beside me. If I made friends, you scared them away. I couldn't even be with Mum and Dad without you breathing down my neck, suffocating me. I didn't have anything or anyone but you, and all I wanted was to escape the hold you'd had on me ever since I could remember. You groomed me into submission as soon as I could talk.'

'You loved me.'

'You told me I did – so much that I believed it. I believed everything you told me. You were always right.'

Maxim fell silent. That terrified her more than if he was yelling.

'Do you know what they did to me, after they sent you away?' she said, talking to the darkness. 'I was sectioned. They had me locked up with crazy people for two years. Isn't that ironic? You raped me and got me pregnant, yet *I* was the one who was locked up. They thought I needed to be saved from myself, that I was going to harm myself, but that Christianity could cure you. I didn't need to be saved from myself, I needed to be saved from *you*.'

'The doctors made you forget me,' he said, as though he hadn't heard a word she had said. 'When I came back from my first posting in the north, you were pregnant with Ryan's baby. I had lost you to him. You weren't the girl I knew anymore, you were a beautiful woman, and you'd forgotten me.

'I waited for you to see sense, to remember everything, but you never did. I watched Chloe grow up, a miniature you, and finally one day I realised: if I couldn't have you, I could have her. She was so much like you, Paige. It was like looking back in time. Although I knew she wouldn't make up for not having you, I thought she could help me fill the void. But even after I had her, I still couldn't forget that she was only a substitute.'

Paige sobbed in the darkness, and thought of all the lives Maxim had destroyed: hers, Chloe's, Ryan's, the lives of their parents.

'You're a monster!'

'You left me no choice! I tried to make you remember. I tried to erase Ryan from your life; I burned his belongings, I cut him from your photos, but still you wouldn't remember. I have spent my entire life watching you and protecting you. I removed everything of Chloe's from her bedroom; I taunted you with the home video to scare you in the hope you would come to me yourself – but you wouldn't, so I burned down the house so you would have to stay here with me. I've done so much for you, and still you won't say that you love me like you used to.'

She hadn't been going mad – *he* was mad and she was his prey. *He* was the man that Ryan wanted dead. Had Ryan tried to kill Maxim with the gun? Could he not go through with it? Or had he been wrong and suspected someone else entirely? Had Ryan really killed himself? Had Maxim used Ryan's gun to kill their father?

The strip lighting flickered on. She began to see flashes of them: Chloe, John, and Mary, sat on chairs with their hands tied behind their backs, duct tape holding their ankles to the chair legs and taped over their mouths. Maxim approached the bed, appearing closer and closer with every flicker of light.

'What are you doing?' Paige cried, shrinking away from him. She felt as powerless as she had all those years ago as she'd waited for her brother to creep along the hall and into her bedroom.

'Taking back what's mine.'

Chloe screamed behind the duct tape as Maxim pulled Paige's ankles so she was lying down on the bed. Paige cried and struggled against him; his hand pressed down on her injured ankle, and then he pinned her down with his body, forcing his mouth onto hers. She bit his lip until blood poured into her mouth. Maxim cried out and pinned her to the bed with one hand around her neck. She freed one leg and launched her knee into his groin.

He doubled over and she thrust the top of her head into his. As he fell limp against her, Paige had to fight away the nausea. Her head throbbed, she was dizzy and felt faint, but she wasn't going to give in. This was her only chance to get free. She spotted his keys on the bed: they had slipped out of his pocket during the struggle.

'Chloe! You have to get free. The keys to the cuffs and the door are right here on the bed.'

Chloe struggled frantically to free herself from the duct tape around her wrist and ankles. The whites of her eyes were red from crying, and she had a purple bruise on her cheek.

'Chloe, move back to back with John and he can free you.'

Chloe nodded, shuffled her chair towards John and manoeuvred round so she was sitting with her back to his.

'John, help your mum out of the tape. Try and be quick, darling, okay?'

Paige watched from the bed, stealing looks at Maxim, who was lying unconscious on top of her.

Maxim began to stir.

John seemed to take forever. Mary was petrified, her big eyes peering around the room while liquid dripped from her seat.

Maxim groaned.

The tape from Chloe's wrist fell to the floor.

'Well done, John!'

Chloe ripped off the tape and instantly went to free her children.

It took precious minutes, and although Maxim wasn't yet conscious, he was beginning to move around.

Once the children were free, Chloe came to the end of the bed.

'Are you okay?' Chloe whispered.

'I'm fine,' Paige lied, feeling dizzy and nauseous. 'The keys are here, by his shoulder.'

'I can't reach.'

'You'll have to climb over him.'

Chloe's complexion paled. 'But what if he wakes up?'

'Chloe, you have to try, he could wake up any moment. This is our only chance!'

Chloe tried to lean over without getting on the bed, but eventually rested a knee on the mattress. She still couldn't reach. In the end she had to climb onto the bed and reach over Maxim, her body inches from his; she grabbed the keys.

'Well done. Now you need to unlock the handcuffs.'

Chloe looked down at Maxim below her, and then at her mother. She reached out towards the handcuffs on Paige's right wrist. After a few misses, the key entered the lock. From the way she had to hold all of her weight on her knees, the key turned painfully slow in the lock. When the lock clicked open, they both sighed with relief.

Chloe took the key out of the lock and shoved the keys in her pocket.

'Well done, Chloe!'

Paige had unclipped her wrist and was beginning to unwrap the tape around the plaster cast when Maxim's eyes snapped open. He spotted Chloe above him and struck her with all his might. The blow sent her flying off the bed and out of sight.

'No!'

Paige wrapped her legs around his torso as he struggled to pin her down. She had started to loosen the tape when Maxim's hand grabbed her free wrist.

'You're not getting out of here, Paige! I'm not losing you again!'

She brought her knee up against his chin and heard a tooth crack. He cried out and let go of her wrist to cup his mouth. She freed the cast, struggled to her feet, and jumped over him. Maxim's hand shot up and grabbed her ankle; she fell halfway off the bed. Paige kicked wildly, and felt the heel of her foot connect with his nose.

As Maxim fell back, Paige dragged herself off the bed and clambered to her feet.

'Come on!' Paige said, ushering Chloe and the children up the stairs. Chloe gave the keys to Paige. Her hands shook as she tried to find the right key for the door. They reached the top of the stairs and she slid the key inside the lock.

'You need to grab the phone in the hallway and get outside. Call 999, and then you need to run. Run down the driveway until you're far away from here. Do you understand?'

Chloe nodded furiously, terrified of leaving her prison for the first time in ten years, with children who had never seen the outside world before.

'You can do this,' Paige said, stroking her daughter's cheek. 'You have to – for Jacob.'

Determination filled Chloe's eyes and she nodded.

'I love you,' Paige said, embracing her quickly before she opened the door.

Her father's body lay on the ground with a gunshot wound in his back, his blood disappearing between the cracks in the floorboards.

Chloe and the children rushed down the hallway, as Paige shut the door to the basement and locked it from the inside.

32

I nearly cried when I heard the voice of the 999 dispatcher on the phone. I told her who I was and what had happened, and to send help to the vicarage in the village. I told her Jacob was at the hospital – the missing boy was mine, and only ended the call when the woman at the other end promised that he would be safe until I got to him.

I ran down the lane with Mary held to me with my good arm, and John running beside me. We all had bare feet, and the gravel bit into our skin. Mary and John were too shocked to speak – Mary was too terrified to run, so I had to carry her. The fresh air and the wide openness of freedom must have felt so alien to them, as they had only ever known their world in the basement. John was crying from the gravel cutting his feet, but he knew we couldn't stop running – he knew we were in danger. John's first experience of the real world was pain and the darkness of night. Both he and Mary had seen my dead grandfather; their naked feet were stained with his blood. Mary clenched her eyes shut, too terrified to see the new world around her, but John's eyes were as wide as they could be, as if he had to take it all in, however scary it was. Tears ran down my cheeks: not from fear, but from sheer relief; after ten miserable years, I was finally free – and Jacob was alive.

'We just need to keep running, John, okay? You're doing so well, I'm so proud of you.'

We ran down the lane, past the tall, looming trees that lined the driveway.

They don't even know what trees are. They must be so confused.

My mother had sacrificed herself to save us. I almost ran back to the door to the basement, to beg her to come back, but I knew that I had to keep going to save my children. I had to get to Jacob.

The sound of sirens cried in the distance, and I sobbed with relief.

'They're coming, John! We're almost there!'

John didn't know who *they* were. Mary had no idea what was going on. But all of us knew that we had escaped the basement.

We're free. We're finally free.

33

axim stood at the bottom of the stairs, looking up at Paige.

She had to give Chloe and the children time to escape. It was her he wanted. Blood poured from his nose and stained his skin and clothes. She had never seen him so angry.

'I just wanted us to be together,' he said, walking up the stairs. 'I just wanted to have my girl back. Why couldn't you let me?' He reached her, standing on the closest step to her, staring deep into her eyes, still towering over her.

'Because you took *my* girl.'

She grabbed his broken nose and twisted it in her hand.

He screamed as she twisted the fractured cartilage. His hands snatched her throat and shoved her against the door. His hold was so tight that she couldn't breathe. Her head felt as though it was going to explode. She tried to free herself, punching at his chest and ribs, and trying to grab his nose again, but he held her at arm's length as he squeezed the life out of her.

She fumbled with the key in the lock on the door and turned it just as her vision began to fade. The door flew open.

As they fell to the floor Maxim lost his grip on her neck. She heaved for air, gasping and holding her swollen throat. Maxim lunged on top of her. They writhed around on the floor in their father's blood, kicking and thrashing, right beside the body. She slammed the heel of her palm into Maxim's broken nose, scrambled up to her feet as he fell back in agony, and ran towards the open front door and into the night.

He chased after her as she ran behind the house, away from the lane where she had told Chloe and the children to go, and headed for the graveyard.

Paige ran blindly through the night. Her bare feet slipped and slid on the dewy grass. Her twisted ankle was slowing her down; the pain was almost unbearable. She could hear Maxim's heavy breathing behind her. He was getting closer, trying to grab at her T-shirt, his fingers grazing against the fluttering fabric.

Paige pushed through the pain and darted through the trees, between the dark trunks, stubbing her toes on their raised roots. She could see the light of the moon reflecting off the windows of the church. Her lungs and throat were burning from the fresh night air and the first bit of exercise she'd had in years. Her traumatised throat continued to swell, allowing less and less air into her lungs. If she kept running she would faint. Her whole body ached from fighting, running, lack of food and sleep. She couldn't keep going for much longer.

Maxim was so close now she could feel the heat of his body and smell the blood from his broken nose.

He used all his weight and strength to shove her straight into a tree trunk. She saw nothing but darkness as she slammed into the tree and collapsed to the ground.

*   *   *

Paige faded in and out of consciousness and felt the scrape of gravel against her back. When her eyes opened briefly, she saw the stars in the night sky. She heard Maxim's groans as he dragged her by her ankles. She coughed and choked every time she tried to breathe.

When she finally came to, she was inside the church, lying on the floor at the top of the aisle. Candles were lit, giving the church a warm glow, but it was freezing. Paige was alone.

Her whole body shook. Her head was aching so much that it brought tears to her eyes. But this wasn't like a migraine: it was more like trauma to her brain. It was as though she could feel it swelling within her skull, pressing against the bone with nowhere to go. She opened her mouth to groan and blood poured from between her lips and splashed onto the floor. She brought her fingertips to her lips, which came away covered in dark, warm blood. With her tongue, she found a gap in her top row of teeth. She spat and spat, but hot blood kept filling her mouth.

She tried to stand but fell to her knees as everything began to spin. Crawling to the nearest pew, she watched her blood drip onto the stone floor. She climbed to her feet and dragged herself along the back of the pew, heading for the door. She pushed herself towards it, stumbled and fell against it, unable to stop everything from spinning. She leaned her head on the door, looked down to the floor, and vomited. She retched bloody bile, trying not to fall backwards. She attempted to open the door with her bloody hands, but couldn't. Maxim had locked her inside.

'Maxim?' Her voice echoed in the tall church.

The organ began to play, each note blaring out. Paige retched again, leaning against the door. The sounds were like hammer blows to her skull. She sobbed and slapped her hands over her ears.

'MAXIM, STOP! PLEASE STOP!'

The church fell silent, and she dared to open her eyes and uncover her ears.

Footsteps sounded up the aisle.

'They'll be checking the house, so we have a little

time,' Maxim said, his voice echoing from somewhere in the church.

The police. They will have saved Chloe and the children. Maybe they'll get here in time to save me.

Maxim came into view. He was wearing his priest's robes and his cheeks were shimmering from tears. Ryan's gun was in his hand.

'It wasn't supposed to happen like this.'

He hooked his arms under hers and dragged her from the doorway.

'We were supposed to have so much time together.' He dragged her down the aisle; a tear fell from his chin and onto her face. 'You would have been happy in the basement with your daughter, your grandchildren, and me.'

All Paige could see were her limp legs and the trail of her own blood. She had no energy to fight back. She could barely keep her eyes open.

'But in death, we can be together forever.'

He is going to kill me.

'Maxim, it's over,' she whispered, blood bubbling on her lips.

'This life will be, but our love will never end. We will carry our love through to the other side, and spend every blissful moment together. You'll see.'

She cried out as he dragged her up the stone steps to the sanctuary.

'It will only hurt for a second, and then we'll both be at peace.'

Maxim sat down with his back to the altar and rested her head on his lap. He looked down at her. She felt the coolness of the gun against her temple.

'I'll shoot you first, and then myself.'

'You won't go to heaven, Maxim,' she whispered. 'You will go to hell for what you've done.'

'The Lord will forgive me.'

'I won't. Even when I'm dead.'

She heard him cock the gun.

'Tell me you love me. Your last words should be that you love me.'

This is it. I'm going to die. He'd rather I die than be free.

'Go to hell.'

A tear dropped from his face and onto hers.

'I love you, Paige. You'll always be my girl.'

The plaster cast cracked against the side of his head and sent white dust and splinters into the air. He dropped the gun as his hands rushed to protect his head.

Paige grabbed the gun and pulled the trigger.

Her brother's face vanished before her eyes, and then everything went dark.

Epilogue

Paige and Chloe strolled down the path from the holiday home on the Dorset coast, their arms linked, while John and Mary ran ahead, their eyes fixed on the sparkling blue sea.

'Be careful!' Chloe called after them, watching them run down the sloping path that led to the sandy beach. They ignored her, too excited to slow down, the backs of their necks white from the sun cream slathered onto them. Jacob let go of Paige's hand and chased after them, calling for them to wait.

'Will I ever stop worrying about them?' Chloe asked her mother.

'Never. I didn't stop worrying about you, even when I thought you were dead.'

Their therapists had recommended the summer getaway. The children needed time to play, to be free, before embarking on their next big journey: school.

Greta and Richard had planned to come on the trip to the south coast, but had both fallen ill with the flu. Ryan's parents had become like her own in the last year; she couldn't have done this without them.

Maxim had left Jacob outside the hospital when he knew he could do nothing else to save him. After Chloe and Jacob were reunited in the hospital, the media went crazy. Helicopters circled above like vultures and barriers kept the reporters fifty feet from the hospital doors. Following their release from hospital, the family were taken into hiding to recover without the world's eyes watching through camera lenses.

Paige had been seeing Robin Higgins, the therapist she had fled from. Given her history, she knew why shrinks scared her now. They had examined her for two long years. Robin helped her deal with her addictions, and she had been clean for almost a year. He helped her to work through the memories of the sexual and mental abuse she suffered during her childhood, and to understand how her brain had protected her for so many years by hiding the memories away. Psychogenic Amnesia and Post-Traumatic Stress Disorder had forced the memories deep within her psyche, so when she had been released from the institution at the age of eighteen, she'd had no recollection of what had put her there.

If she had remembered what had happened to her, she would have never have let Maxim anywhere near Chloe.

Paige still wondered why she hadn't sensed that her daughter was hidden beneath his floorboards: shouldn't mother's intuition have told her something?

Maxim had ruined her life. The childhood abuse had rewired her brain and had distorted her view of the world. Even after she was free of him, she still hadn't made any friends; she had isolated herself because it was all she knew.

Now he was gone, and the truth was out, she could finally begin to heal. She may not have done the right thing when she had the chance, but she did in the end: Maxim was dead. He couldn't hurt them anymore.

'I envy them,' Chloe said, her red hair dancing in the wind. 'They have come so far in the last year, and I'm still so stuck.'

'Children are different, Chloe. They're more adaptable than adults. And they didn't face all of the abuse you did. You've accomplished much more than you think. You surprise me every day.'

Paige and Chloe had only just stopped sharing a bed at night. Their therapists had decided it was time. Neither of them wanted it, but they both knew deep down that it couldn't go on forever. They left their bedroom doors open at night, and had their beds facing the doorways, so they could look up and check that the other was still there, that they hadn't been separated again.

The ASBO tag around Paige's right ankle had been

removed a week before their trip to Dorset. The judge had ordered her to wear it for over six months, and she continued to have monthly blood tests to prove that she wasn't drinking.

'How does it feel?' Paige asked as she looked at her daughter, the sun on her milky skin and the sea breeze playing with her hair. Her hair had been cut to her shoulders, just like she'd wanted all those years ago before she was taken.

My girl is so beautiful.

'It's as though I have died and gone to heaven.'

To their left they could see the sprawling cliffs and a ribbon of yellow beach. In front of them was the horizon, where the dark sea stretched out to meet the bright blue sky.

'Let's run,' Paige said.

'What?'

'Run in the open, in the breeze, in the sun. You're free, Chloe. You need to feel it.'

Chloe looked cautious.

'Come on. I bet I can beat you to the bottom.'

Paige ran down the path, feeling a smile spread across her face. She turned to see Chloe running too with a smile on her face. They ran down the slanted path that zigzagged down the hill until they reached the hot, yellow sand and fell onto their backs, panting and laughing.

'I told you I'd win.'

'You got a head start,' Chloe replied, her chest rising and falling fast.

They looked up at the clear blue sky, and heard the children running towards them. They sat up and greeted them.

'Sit down and take your shoes off,' Paige said, patting the sand beside her. 'You need to feel the sand between your toes.'

Paige and Chloe took off their shoes, and the children copied them, Jacob needing help with his. As they felt the sand between their toes, the children beamed with such surprise that it brought tears to Paige's eyes.

'Shall we race to the water?' Chloe said.

'You four race, I'll judge. I'm knackered after winning the last one.'

'You're just scared I'll beat you this time.' Chloe laughed and got to her feet. 'Right, you three, ready?'

Paige counted down from three and watched them run down the beach towards the sparkling water.

Maybe I am dead, she thought to herself. *Maybe this is heaven.*

After a lifetime of misery, she was finally happy. She watched her daughter and three grandchildren run into the cold sea and gasp at the chill; they kicked and splashed water at each other, smiling the entire time.

Paige rested her hand beside her, and looked to the empty space. Ryan should have been with her, witnessing the beauty that she was so lucky to see. That was how she knew that she wasn't dead; if this was heaven, if it really did exist, he would have been there with them – wasn't that how heaven worked?

Every night, before she fell asleep, she always had the same thought: *If only Ryan hadn't killed himself, he would have been able to see his daughter again.*

She never discovered who it was that Ryan had wanted dead. She liked to think that he had suspected Maxim, that he had got it right, but that he couldn't go through with killing him. Instead, he had ended his own life, unable to face the cruel world anymore. Sometimes, she worried that perhaps Ryan had killed the wrong man, and then killed himself for the error. She often dreamt that Maxim was responsible for Ryan's death somehow. But she couldn't think of that anymore. Maxim was dead – she had stopped him. She was finally free of him: they all were. She had to leave her past behind and focus on the present, her family, their future.

She looked out at Chloe and the children as they splashed about in the water, and realised how lucky she was. Chloe looked to her mother on the beach and beckoned for her to join them, and the children shouted out for her.

Paige wiped her cheeks from tears, got to her feet, and raced towards the water.

Did you enjoy *My Girl*?
Leave a review!

Thank you so much for choosing to read *My Girl*.

If you enjoyed *My Girl*, it would be great if you could post a review on Amazon (and if you're addicted to Goodreads like I am, a review would be fantastic there too!). We may not judge a book by its cover, but we do judge a book by its reviews. Spreading the word by leaving a review inspires others to choose *My Girl* as their next read! I would love to hear what you thought of the book. Thank you so much for all of your support!

All the best,

Jack

Acknowledgements

First of all, I would like to thank *you* for reading this book. By holding this story in your hands, you are helping to make this author's dream a reality.

Thank you to Averill Buchanan for your editorial help and advice, and for working to a tight deadline – you're great. Thank you to Sarah Nisbet for your sharp eye for detail when proofreading this book, and for all of your great feedback – you're a star. Thank you to Emma J Hardy for creating the book cover of my dreams!

I would like to thank all of the amazing book bloggers who helped spread the word about this book.

I couldn't have delivered my second book without the undying support and love of my biggest fans: Sandra Yuill, Pamela Jordan, and Luke Holdaway. Thank you for everything. I'd also like to thank everyone else who has inspired me to follow my dreams and never give up.

About the Author

Jack Jordan lives in East Anglia, England. He is an introvert disguised as an extrovert, an intelligent man who can say very unintelligent things, and a self-confessed bibliomaniac with more books than sense.

To find out more about Jack, check for updates on future projects, read some of his social media ramblings or get in touch, visit:

 www.twitter.com/_JackJordan_

 www.facebook.com/JackJordanOfficial

 www.goodreads.com/jackjordan

 www.instagram.com/JackJordan_author

www.jackjordanofficial.co.uk

If you enjoyed *My Girl*, read the first chapter of Jack Jordan's debut thriller…

ANYTHING
FOR HER

1

Louise had never wanted her husband to die. Not until he ripped their family apart.

Testicular cancer? Rabies? A fatal fall from a windy clifftop? Lightning strike to his adulterous crotch? She hadn't decided. All she knew was, once a husband told his wife that he had been having an affair with her younger sister, it was more than acceptable, if not entirely necessary, for his wife to imagine his gruesome death over and over for her own pleasure.

They had argued all night: ever since Michael had confessed to the ten-month affair. Just as she was drifting off to sleep, he divulged.

'I've been sleeping with Denise.'

She instantly forgot to how to breathe.

'I love you, Louise. I don't want our marriage to end because of this.'

Her throat constricted. Her heart was beating wildly in her chest.

'I… I don't understand.'

'I've been meaning to tell you—'

'No,' she turned to face him. 'Say it again. Look into my eyes and say it again.'

She stared at her husband's bewitching face, and waited for him to explain that it was a sick prank. He would laugh hysterically as her mouth relaxed into a relieved smirk and she would slap his arm playfully. *You really got me for a moment there, Mike!*

'I've been having an affair with your sister.'

Michael's complexion paled as he watched his words sink in.

He was lying – he had to be. Michael wouldn't do that. Maybe she had fallen asleep; maybe she was having a nightmare. Was it possible for her to feel her heart break while she slept?

Her eyes began to sting with tears. She couldn't escape the thought of her husband writhing naked on top of her sister, both of them glistening with sweat and panting like excited dogs; she imagined Denise clutching her husband's buttocks as he slammed into her, while Michael caressed her breast with his hand as the gold wedding ring on his finger cooled her nipple.

Louise got out of bed, rushed to the en-suite, and vomited.

*　　*　　*

After an exhausting night of tears, yelling, apologies, and expletives, they occupied the room in stifling silence, with every word they had spoken echoing in their ears. Louise sat on the end of the bed – the side of their marital bed that she had occupied for twenty years.

She looked out of the window, as the sun rose and began to warm the December frost that sparkled on the London rooftops, and wondered if she would ever be able to look at her husband again without wishing him dead.

Michael stood at the foot of the bed with the facial expression of a scolded child. His bottom lip quivered as he tried to keep the tears at bay.

'Why, Michael?' she asked weakly. 'Why my sister, of all people?'

'I… I couldn't handle the secrets any more. I couldn't handle the distance you put between us. Denise came on to me and I let her.'

'It seems we all have secrets,' she replied, her eyes fixed on the window. 'But don't worry, my secrets don't involve fucking your brother.'

They succumbed to the silence again. Louise looked down at the hastily packed suitcase by her feet. She had to escape her new, agonising reality before it killed her.

'So not only have you destroyed your business, lost all of our money, and destroyed our family, but you've decimated our marriage and severed my bond with my sister forever.'

She looked at him with tears in her eyes, a woman too weak to take another knock.

'I will never forgive myself.'

'I will never forgive you either.'

Tears ran down her cheeks and reflected the rising sun in their streams.

She stood and reached down for the suitcase handle; fresh tears dropped to the carpet.

'Please stay. Please stay until we work this out.'

'I can't bear to be near you right now,' she walked to the door. 'I can't even look at you.'

She opened the bedroom door while Michael sobbed behind her. In front of her stood their two children.

Ten-year-old Dominic looked startled to see his mother's worn complexion and bloodshot eyes. His small hands were shaking.

Eighteen-year-old Brooke, a youthful double of her mother, stood next to him; her cheeks were streaked with dried tears.

Both children looked utterly drained, as though neither of them had slept a wink. They must have listened to every word.

'I need to go away for a while,' she said, wiping tears from her face.

'Can we come with you?' Dominic asked.

'No, darling. Mummy needs some time to herself for a few days.' She knelt down in front of her son; his eyes shimmered with hurt. 'That doesn't mean I don't need you or love you with every part of me. It just means that I need to go away and have a good, long think. Okay?'

'What have you got to think about?'

'Not very nice things. But whenever I need cheering up, I'll think of you.'

'You promise you'll come back?'

Tears began to fill his eyes.

'I promise you, my angel. I'll be back.'

Louise spread her arms and her son fell into her chest and unfurled his sobs. She held him to her, her heart breaking all over again, and looked up at Brooke.

Our secret did this.

She didn't need to say it out loud. Brooke knew.

Louise gave her son one last squeeze and a kiss before she got to her feet to stand before her eldest child. She entered into a tight embrace with her and kissed her quickly on the cheek.

'Be strong,' she whispered into her daughter's ear. 'Be strong for your brother.'

From the top of the South Kensington townhouse, Louise carried the heavy suitcase down each flight of stairs, trying to ignore the approaching steps of her husband, and the children following behind him like his shadow.

'Don't go. Please don't leave me.'

Louise couldn't trust herself to reply without crying; she hurried for the last flight of stairs. The suitcase strained her arm and back, but she didn't care: the sooner she escaped, the better.

When she reached the front door, she stopped in her tracks. Michael stood on the bottom step of the staircase; the children remained at the top. Louise couldn't take her eyes away from the framed photo hanging proudly by the door for all to see: the photo of her and Michael on their wedding day. Standing next to her was Denise in her maid of honour dress; Michael's brother, the best man, stood to the right. The four of them were laughing. Their wide grins radiated glee and wedding-day beauty. She had never noticed that Michael and Denise's eyes were locked, frozen by the click of the camera.

Rage swelled in her chest. Her entire body shook with hate, and her skin flushed hot. She dropped the suitcase with a bang, snatched the photo frame from the wall, and launched it at her husband with a scream. He ducked as it crashed against the wall and exploded into shards of glass and splinters of wood.

Dominic screamed from the top of the stairs and ran out of sight.

Louise looked at the scene, at the mess that her life had become, torn between hurting her husband further and running to his aid. She took her keys from the sideboard, picked up her suitcase, and rushed out of the house, slamming the door behind her. The sound reverberated through the house and sent shudders through those she left behind.

Dive straight into your next thriller: get your copy of *Anything for Her* on Amazon

Printed in Great Britain
by Amazon